.

'Dancing With Spiders'

by

Bernie Walsh

Bloomington, IN

authorHOUSE®

Milton Keynes, UK

AuthorHouse™
1663 Liberty Drive, Suite 200
Bloomington, IN 47403
www.authorhouse.com
Phone: 1-800-839-8640

AuthorHouse™ UK Ltd.
500 Avebury Boulevard
Central Milton Keynes, MK9 2BE
www.authorhouse.co.uk
Phone: 08001974150

First published by AuthorHouse 11/28/2006

ISBN: 978-1-4259-5396-6 (sc)

Printed in the United States of America
Bloomington, Indiana

This book is printed on acid-free paper.

To My Wife Liz

Foreword

My inspirations for this book originate from the cavities of humour rich with characters, some of whom exist in real life, blunt but infectious, while others belong to fiction but are nonetheless familiar. The people, whether in the fictional village of Coxburn, amidst the once vibrant Durham coal communities, or in the coastal resort of Benamedina on the Costa del Sol provide a stark contrast.

Harry Farmer, Dave Warlord and Victor Plumtree do exist and in real life are known as Barry, Dave and Colin. It was one night over the Christmas period in 2003 that this story was conceived; Barry being the main protagonist.

I am indebted to Barry Flockett, Dave Wharrior and Colin Wood and to the many people of my home village of Coxhoe, who have contributed to this book and brought about its realisation.

Writing this book has been something of a journey. It was written at a time when my soul was deep and self-pity would have been such an easy option to succumb to. Instead, I was surrounded by an array of characters who ignited a flame. A story was born.

'Dancing with Spiders' evokes a number of emotions; humour is mixed with suspense and tragedy. The two worlds; the north east culture epitomised by the village of Coxburn and the workmen's club at it's hub, contrasting with the Andalucian backdrop, the sun drenched white villas and the scent of flowers.

Combining cultures lies a bed of deception and greed, an unwinding comedy thriller.

～

Harry Farmer is always looking for the action. Since leaving the Army he has always looked for the big opportunity. He thrives on life in the fast lane. Harry likes the lavish life style and has an appetite for women.

His roots lie in the modest but sometimes ruthless shadows of the Durham coalfields in the North east of England. It is there that his friends Dave Warlord and Victor Plumtree hold together an organization that exists for those who need to know, but is unknown to anyone else.

Loyalty is at a premium. Coxburn Retail Union and the death of their financial wizard, Victor Plumtree shows there are seedy elements at work within the organisation. Or is there a third party lurking in the shadows.

Warlord is a worried man. He relied on Plumtree and Farmer. Farmer is off in Spain enjoying the high life and Warlord is feeling vulnerable.

Can Harry Farmer get the right result and does it mean the end of CRU, or can it be saved and move on to more lucrative markets and can they survive the lurid aftertaste?

Chapter 1
Setting the Plan

Harry was standing at the crowded bar looking at his near empty glass. The ice lodged in the bottom of his glass had melted where the vodka had penetrated. Ready to order another he anticipated his latest project.

A wry smile appeared with a comment aimed at camouflage.

"What do ya think TRM means?", Harry chuckled.

"The Royal Marines?", shouted an excited punter.

Harry had a captive audience. He liked that. Being the centre of attention and at the pulse of the action. This was familiar territory.

Bernie Walsh

"I am TRM… The run machine", he teased, referring to his feats on the cricket pitch.

Harry had been a committed military man, working up the ranks, graduating to commander. Strategy and risk were power for the course. He did not have the outward appearance of a soldier but that was deliberate. He was fit and had dexterity. He blended privacy with life in the fast lane like the iced vodka he sipped pensively. A gush to the back of the throat

Amidst the smoke screen bellowing across the bar, there were the wisecracks. No subtlety here. Raw and undiluted humour. If you were offended well that was just bad luck.

Harry felt comfortable in his hometown bar but he was ready for action. The next assignment had already developed and the final planning was underway. But no one would know until the final execution, the target in place and the consignment delivered.

Ambling between the crowds, Harry's personality was electric at times! A fusing extravert, but there was also an entrepreneur at work.

Harry was at his best with a crowd around him but this assignment was private and solitary, like so many military maneuvers and he was his own man. Precision Farmer was at work.

By the end of the month he would be sipping quality vodka in the Greek Islands. The rich life and all the trimmings would unfold. The woman in his life at his side clad in suntan and little else. Harry enjoys the fast lane and women need to be in overdrive as well.

Harry's mind was racing, beads of sweat were appearing on his forehead. Adrenaline, not anxiety pounding away. He pondered his trip to Spain. There was excitement and anticipation.

Harry's plan was more devious and certainly more dangerous than the 'scams' associated with the CRU. The CRU had been importing tobacco and liquor and selling it on for a tidy profit. This was piecemeal to what Harry contemplated.

Returning home he packed a small bag, just the essentials and headed for the airport.

Newcastle was a mere two hours flight time from Malaga and the army of British compatriots. His 'Easy-Jet' ticket provided him a seat but no complimentary meal or drink. That would come later he pondered.

Harry was asleep most of the flight, waking to the screeching breaks and bump of the descended plane. The surge forward by eager passengers to the waiting buses took no time and within 20 minutes harry was heading in a taxi for a hotel – the 'Rio Grande' in Belamedina.

The hotel was a place he knew well. The owner Clive Lomas was British, an ex-Royal Engineers Major and his petite wife, Nardina had met him during a posting to Gibraltar 10 years earlier. He knew Harry from their early days in the Army and their friendship continued when they hit 'civvi' street.

Clive had a slender build and did not carry much weight. In recent years he had acquired a beard. A secretive man, Clive had worked with Harry on a number of missions.

Clive left the Army and used his pension on buying the 'Rio Grande'. But the small and friendly hotel was a 'front' for more sinister activities.

Like Harry, Clive had a sharp mind. They were up to all kinds of enterprise but Harry had humour. Clive was stubborn and hid his emotions deep just like his business activities.

Clive had some ideas about a bigger operation; more fish in a bigger pond!

Harry's best friend, Warlord was always won over to Harry's ideas, particularly when the cash came rolling in but he was sceptical about what Harry had in mind this time. But Harry had persuasive charms and he knew he could convince Warlord that his ideas would pay dividends. All it would take time would be time and patience and Warlord would come round to the 'Plan' Harry thought.

Nardina was a former singer and dancer, whose family had land and property but they did not encourage her choice of career. It was Nardina's choice to be independent. She was a natural beauty with all the Mediterranean features. But she was vulnerable and her apparent vivacious personality hid insecurity.

Nardina had a glimpse of Harry as he came into reception.

"Si Harryee", Nardina shouted, almost singing his name.

"Hiya Nardi", Harry whispered in a noticeable North of England dialect, as he gazed at her tender frame and piercing eyes.

"Where's Clive?, he inquired.

"He's gonna fishin', always fishin'". She smiled gently, kissing Harry firmly on the lips.

Harry got the signals clearly but Clive was a mate and mates don't play with each other's wives, not that Harry was in wedded bliss, but Clive might be back with a catch soon.

Harry had customary vodka and ice at the hotel bar and headed for his room on the second floor. The room was spacious and airy with a small balcony overlooking the beach and harbour. Harry looked out onto the main street. Groups of people staggered home from the restaurants and bars, not noisily but with good humour.

It was after 1 am and Harry wanted some sleep but decided on a shower. As he glanced into the cubicle he saw the outline of a body. Much to his disappointment, it was not a vivacious blonde or brunette but a quite motionless frame of a man, slumped with his face down on the tiled floor. There was no blood but as he pulled over the body towards him, he gasped in amazement.

"Victor Plumtree", he spluttered. Victor was another military exile, who was involved in running his own security firm. The EU had opened up markets for him, well it did. The only journey for Victor now would be the morgue, thought Harry.

Harry was shocked and bemused. What was Victor Plumtree doing in Spain?

He should be in Durham, he thought.

Above all else, Harry did not want a corpse to get in the way of his business venture but the local 'Policia' would want to know all kinds – questions and more questions. What should he do?

Harry didn't panic. He called reception, hoping to get Nardina. Instead he got Sanchez, the night porter, who had been drinking, probably the remains of the sangria.

There was no sign of Nardina. Harry decided to go out for a walk. As he headed for the landing, he heard a hushed voice. It was Nardina.

"Harryee", she whispered, come here.

Harry responded. Nardina led him into a private suite, she and Clive had in the hotel. Clive had not returned from his fishing trip.

Nardina was in a loose fitting dressing gown revealing a natural tanned body. She smiled generously at Harry. It was an inviting smile.

"Where's Clive, Nardi?", Harry inquired.

Hunching her shoulders, Nardina replied

"I don't know. He care more about fishin' than me".

"Harryee, I need to be loved".

A tear appeared her on her olive cheeks. Harry held her close and felt the rhythm of her heart racing. He was feeling quite elated himself.

Kissing seemed inevitable. Nardina kissed him hard on the lips. He responded and passionate kissing continued as they undressed in the bedroom.

Suddenly, there was a knock at the door.

"Policia", there followed a louder thud.

Nardina, with her gown hiding her naked body, rushed to the door.

Opening the door, she gazed at the young officer who spoke in hurried Spanish. The only word Harry could understand was "Clive".

Nardina burst into tears and her emotions were high. She rushed to Clive sobbing

"Clive is a dead"

"Found him dead in the boat. No one else about!".

Harry needed the events of the last two hours like a hole in his head. What was happening. More to the point, with a dead body upstairs and now Clive's death, what could he do?

Nardina was very distressed. She needed him. But what about the consignment in Granada!.

Nardina was sobbing. Harry couldn't handle emotion very well. He was normally controlled but he needed to console his friend's wife. Minutes before they were in passionate embrace but now she needed different emotions.

~

The electronic clock facing down from the imposing flight schedules fascia at Malaga Airport clicked to 21.37. The airport was busy but not hectic. A group of children lingered at the McDonalds stand and three nuns stared in disbelief at their manners.

Couples embracing in anticipation of the departures, others just were embracing after a romantic break awaiting the flight back home. A steady flow of customers headed for the 'duty free' shops. Others mingled. But the man with the athletic frame stood motionless. He was looking for Harry Farmer.

At the checkout there was distinctly shifty woman in a dark skirt and black tights. She suspected something, or was it just the characteristics of a tired and tedious operator frustrated with routine.

Airports were on high alert now since September 11. Everyone was more vigilant and this included Harry. Not unduly worried but keen to scent the seal on his consignment bound for the CRU.

Harry, Warlord, Plumtree and a group of associates in the mid-eighties had formed Coxburn Retail Union. Jokingly it was referred to as the 'local Mafia' but there was a darker side!

His eyes peered but not conspicuously, just sufficient to see the image of a security guards. Harry pensive in anticipation of what he hoped would be the start of a lucrative venture, made a quick call on his mobile.

Flicking open the Vodafone he rang Warlord, a long time school friends, but the go-between in the transaction. Warlord was one of the most inconspicuous characters you could meet. More inclined to be a man of physical endurance when he was a working miner in Durham, than the bulging frame enhanced by beer and fish and chips, he had a pleasing and casual manner.

"Worrie", Harry whispered into the phone.

"Is everything goin' to plan?"

Warlord detected a slight anxiety in Harry's voice.

"Don't worry man, no one suspects anythin', shouted Warlord.

The two men were excited, just like when they were at school, caught up in many antics and exploits.

"Hey, don't worry Harry, the deal's in the bag", blurted Warlord.

"What's this about the 'Plum', hear he's dead?"

Harry went cold for a few seconds. How did Warlord know that?

~

In Durham, the small village church was somber. Victor Plumtree's body was still slumped in the shower cubicle of the Rio Grande Hotel in Belamedina but news of his death hit the local village. They had a lot at stake!

Victor was a popular and trusted man in the community. No one suspected him of anything shady. His trip to Spain had been a last minute decision. Why had he gone?

The service at the parish church had amassed great interest. It was not Victor's wake that would come later in his beloved club, it was a service to remember a great man. His young wife, Vicky was they're sobbing and being consoled by the couple's many friends. Vicky was bemused by Victor's disappearance.

～

Nardina was lying on top of the bed. The bright sunshine radiated heat to her oily body. She had not seen Harry for two days and wanted him to console her. Clive's death had hit her hard. They had been together for 10 years. It was not always easy and their relationship was not without the odd derailment. Both had played the field. It was fair to say their relationship was on the rocks!

Clive was 10 years older than Nardina. In her mid thirties, Nardina was glamorous without make up and with a hint of lipstick and mascara she was an icon. She had many an admiring gigolo and she knew how to turn up the heat. Passion oozed from her veins.

Nardina appeared disinterested in Clive's fishing trips but deep down she was suspicious. He had acquired some wealth, coming to Spain with his Army gratuity but he rarely, if ever bestowed any generosity upon Nardina. There was something sinister about Clive's fishing trips and his death deepened the sense of mystery.

Harry had returned from the airport, he did not want to hang around too much for fear that this would alert suspicious officials. He caught Sanchez at the bar serving drinks.

"Sancho. I'll have a vodka and ice si? ", Harry's eyes glanced upward, as if in a military parade.

"One minute Signor, I get yur drink!

Sancho looked particularly dirty today. Unshaven, with several days' growth and his greasy hair looking forlorn, there was an odour of stale cigar smoke and garlic.

Sanchez brought a tall tumbler half filled with Vodka and a hint of tonic and ice. Harry sipped it quenching hard on the glass rim.

"Sancho, get me another drink", Harry felt a ripple across the collar of his shirt. The long finger nails digging into his neck.

Sancho brought the drink. Harry looked around and there gazing into his eyes was Nardina, eyes sharp and body illuminated by her bright pink dress.

"Harryée, where have you been hidin'", she hugged him close. Harry did not retreat, as the two clung together. There was chemistry between them and a passion as they embraced.

Nardina whispered in Harry's right ear.

"Harryee, come upstairs. I have some vodka and have what you want, si", she grabbed his arm.

Harry followed the dark haired beauty up to her apartment situated on the second floor but at the side of the hotel. There was a private balcony and terrace overlooking part of the beach, but it was secluded.

The sun outside was scorching, in the eighties and rising. The apartment was a pale green and lemon décor and the furniture was light oak. It was roomy and the air conditioning provided a cool breeze.

A four poster bed, which had a fine net cover as protection against mosquito invasion, dominated the bedroom, but no one would invade Nardina and Harry for their afternoon of cavorting. Harry was interrupted once but there would be no distractions this time.

As he kissed Nardina hard on the lips their emotions had no rationale. They were rampant in their lovemaking.

"Harryee, I want you to make me scream love", she panted, as Harry undid a low cut bra. She already had his trousers undone and their bodies clung together. They clambered for the giant size bed; both naked and kissing incessantly there bodies exposed.

The ring tone on Harry's mobile phone seemed distant as they rose in ecstasy and elation. But Harry felt that at least for a minute he might have to compromise. He enjoyed caressing Nardina, but a brief interlude was necessary.

Warlord was at the end of the phone, increasingly impatient in his tone.

"Harry man, there are problems, where are ya?", he was agitated.

"In bliss mate, that's where", joked Harry.

Warlord was not in a humorous mood. In his blunt North of England dialect, he blurted.

"Where the fuckin hell is bliss?

Harry wanted to laugh but he knew what Warlord was like.

"Listen Dave, don't worry, what's wrong?" Harry tried to calm his friend.

Warlord was unrestrained.

"Harry man they are onto us", he sounded a worried man, breathing heavily.

"What do you mean Dave?", Harry was more sedate now.

"I know who killed Victor Plum Harry, honest!" Dave Warlord's voice was resolved.

"Who Worrie, who …….?, demanded Harry.

Harry was lying with his back to Nardine. They were both in transit and a passionate afternoon was on hold.

There was a silence at the end of the phone. Harry wanted to know more but he was keen to get back to Nardina, who was kissing his back and he felt elated again.

"Who Worrie, who ....?, Harry was becoming impatient with his close friend.

Warlord retorted.

"Clive man, Clive. He killed him, the bastard" The CRU's not chuffed. Victor was their main guy, you know that Harry don't ya, eh.

"Give me a bit of time Worrie. Dave doesn't do anything. I'll get back to you soon. Give me an hour or so, okay!"

Warlord relented.

"Okay, Harry, you're the boss but remember there's some unhappy people over here, right!

"Okay", Harry reassured his friend, at least for the time being.

He turned to his Latin lover and they disappeared under the covers, rigging in excited laughter.

Harry was thinking in parallel about the immediate satisfaction and a hungry young woman, but he would need to talk to Nardina once their hormones allowed some respite. For the moment, there was ecstasy and the thrills of a woman, who showed no relenting in her demands. Harry was happy but he also pondered his next move.

～

Nightfall drove in fast in Belamedina and as the two lovers slept, there was rustling on the terrace outside. Harry was not a deep sleeper and he crept out of bed. He didn't wish to disturb Nardina. He untangled her arms from his thighs, put on a robe and unlocked the patio door.

The click of the door lock disturbed the intruder. Harry did some surveillance. There was no one around.

He crept back into the room. Nardina was still sleeping. Harry got clothed and decided to visit his room.

He switched on the light, it flickered and then there was a full burst of light. The door leading out to the small balcony was open and the net curtain flowed slightly. The bed was untouched. Clean linen. There was a light on in the bathroom. Harry went in and to his amazement; Victor Plum's body had gone. There was no sign of blood or anything. The floor was clean.

As Harry went to leave the bathroom he felt a hand on his harm. It was Nardina.

"Harryee, you leave me, I want your love tonight in my bed, si". She held his hand tight and gazed into his eyes. Harry was mesmerized by her seductive glance. But he wanted to talk to Nardina.

Harry needed answers to questions and he hoped Nardina could provide the answers.

Nardina could see that Harry was pre-occupied. She wondered why he had discarded her.

"Harryee", Nardina held her head close to Harry's shoulder.

"What is wrong, you don't like me anymore!" Nardina was crying, tears rolled down her cheeks.

Harry held her close.

"Listen Nardi, I love being with you and I want to make love to you again and again but I need to know something". Harry's facial expression was calm but determined.

" Did you know what Clive was up to when he went fishing, Nardi?" Harry was never subtle when asking questions. Diplomacy came second to directness.

Nardina looked Harry straight in the eye. She looked puzzled by his question.

❧

"I don't know what ya mean Harryee". Nardina's response seemed genuine.

Harry was keen to know how much Nardina actually knew about Clive's activities.

"Nardi, what do you know about Victor Plumtree?"

Nardina looked distressed.

"He the man from Durham", she whimpered.

"Yeah, he is a friend of mine". Harry was getting a little agitated.

Nardina continued without any further prompting from Harry.

"He is dead and Clive said he found him in your room Harryee", Nardina was quite forceful but her voice was wavering.

"Wait a minute Nardi, what do you mean, my room".

"Clive told me the morning you arrived that this man Victor was in the shower and he was dead".

Nardina's response did not satisfy Harry who felt that he was somehow in the frame. It was obvious someone had murdered Victor before Harry arrived at the 'Rio Grande'.

Harry's mind was in overdrive. Other than Clive, who knew about Victor's death and the whereabouts of his body? Now, Clive was dead, was there a link?

Chapter 2
Dancing Spiders

Harry awoke to the din of the Benalmedina resort trade. He could hear a gabble of voices outside.

There were English voices. Probably Essex Harry thought, or certainly the southeast. Voices intermingled with German and Dutch. It was mid morning and the smell of food was quite mouth-watering. Harry always had an enormous appetite after a night of sex and Nardina had generated a feast.

Harry turned over in bed but Nardina had gone, only the imprint of her slender body was evident on the ruffled sheets.

As Harry wandered over to the patio window, a gentle breeze calmed the humidity. The door opened. Vibrant and vivacious, Nardina entered the room carrying a tray, with a pot of coffee, croissants, toast and bacon and eggs.

"Good morning darling. You sleep well Harryee?", she had a tight red dress that barely covered the top of her long legs.

"When you let me Nardi, you know what a man wants. He took the tray from her, placing it on a table look out of the patio window. Harry discarded the croissants and picked up a plate of bacon and eggs.

Taking a bite from some buttered toast, Harry looked across at Nardina. She was sipping some black coffee and nibbling the edge of a croissant.

"You got up early Nardi, going off me". Harry had a wry smile.

"Harryee", she said with a two-tone voice, her face was a constant smile.

"You tease me darling". She moved her body closer to him, rubbing her thigh against his.

"Listen, why don't we go out this afternoon. We go for a drive, or whatever you want?"

"Si?", her eyes were focussed on Harry, like a moving target.

"Nardi, there are things I need to sort out first".

"Yes we'll go out and enjoy the sun!".

Harry wanted nothing more than to be with Nardi but he also had to find out what had happened to Clive and Victor. Warlord would be ringing and he would be looking for some answers.

Warlord was a good friend, Harry was not frightened of him but they respected each other, as they did when they were young footballers.

Harry thought about the events of the last few days. His mind also concentrated on the night an intruder was roaming around outside on the terrace. He wondered if Nardi knew anything more than she was letting on about.

Harry raised his arms high above his head. He walked towards the shower cubicle. No surprises this time he thought. The cool spray of water rinsed away the perspiration and for the moment he felt invigorated. He was about to switch off the shower but as he turned around, he glanced at an advancing body. It was difficult to make out who it was. They were fast and furious. Harry felt something cold, like metal.

Harry was not dead, but he was unconscious.

Warlord was knocking out Harry's mobile phone number.

"I hate these bloody things" he muttered to himself". He didn't realize that he had Harry's number logged in his mobile.

"No reply, where the hell is he?". Warlord was brash but deep down he was worried about his best friend.

~

Nardi entered the bedroom. She shouted for Harry but there was no answer.

"Harryee, where are you". She looked around the apartment. As she went into the bathroom, she heard a groan.

Quickly and with shock in her face, she gasped when she saw Harry lying there. It was not the sight of his naked body, as she adored lying beside him. It was seeing his body, lifeless and some blood from a head wound.

Nardi knelt down close to him. She put her hand on his head and spoke gently.

"Harryee, darling I didn't know, didn't know about anything, but this man he….".

Harry's eyes flinched and then shot open. He was a little bewildered and confused as he tried to get on his feet.

Holding on to Nardina, he shook her firmly.

"Nardi, what's going on". He had heard her words, as he came around.

" I get you a drink Harryee. Then we talk I promise you". She was shaking and there were tears in her eyes.

"Clive", Nardina was holding Harry close to her. Teardrops falling on his blue sports shirt, she told him of her fear.

Nardina was trembling. She was pre-occupied, but Harry wanted answers.

The woman in a bright red dress and long black leather coat had arrived at Malaga Airport on the midday flight from Newcastle. On the surface she seemed sophisticated. But she had a brash style and was flamboyant. She edged her way through the crowded arrival terminal into a taxi and headed for the Hotel Rio Grande in Belamedina.

Pressing the brass bell situated at the corner of the light oak counter, she looked up sternly at Sanchez.

"Hola !", he sounded monotone.

"I have a reservation here, my name is Victoria Plumtree". She did not elaborate. Sanchez took the customary details, together with a copy of her passport.

"Room 24 on the second floor, Signorita", Sanchez then went to help with her cases.

"It's okay", said the woman as she walked away to her room.

~

Nardina and Harry were leaving the bedroom as Victoria turned the corner from the lift.

"Vicky, where did you come from?", surprised, Harry stumbled over his words.

"To see what's going on and what happened to Vic. Warlord is hopping mad with you Harry. What the hell is going on Harry?"

"Vicky this is Nardina, Clive's wife. He is also dead, a few days after Victor. There could be a connection". The two women looked at each other, a glance that was not warm but suggested they had something in common. Vicky's guard was up!

The transparency was evident.

Without comment Vicky went on to her room.

Harry wondered why Vicky had traveled over from Durham. Did she know something and why did Warlord not trust him. His best friend didn't trust him. This hurt Harry and despite his tenacity he was close to Warlord. What had changed, he thought?

∿

Nardina and Harry went out for a drive. Apart from their sexual encounters, Nardina felt comfortable with Harry. She trusted him. Harry trusted nobody. He did like being with Nardina but he did not feel at ease with himself, let alone the woman who had become his lover.

The two lovers made their way in Nardi's bright red 'open-top' BMW down a winding bend. Ahead the peninsula. Ahead of them were the towered hotel blocks and mixture of coloured villas up in the mountains. The sun was bright and hot. For many islanders it was 'siesta' time. But siesta was not on Harry's mind.

High above the landscape, Nardina pondered, bringing the car to a sudden halt. For most of the journey, Harry had been quiet, taking in the scenery. Nardina thought it unusual for Harry to be so subdued.

"Harryee, what's wrong wit' you, are you okay?".

Harry didn't answer immediately. His temple tightened.

"Nardina, you know what happened to Victor and Clive don't you. You know….". Before Harry said anything else, Nardina interrupted.

"I killed Clive and Victor, he knew too much". Nardina blurted out a confession that to Harry seemed false. He didn't show any reaction.

"Harryee, did you hear me?"

"I killed them, what are you gonna do?

Harry pulled her towards him and looked into her eyes.

"Nardi, I don't believe you. I know you know who murdered them. You got to be even with me.

Nardina's tears presented an obstacle. Harry felt that Nardi was holding back and leading him on. He was not happy.

Harry walked off down a sandy path, leaving Nardina in the car.

He looked across the landscape. The sun was scorching and a blanket of haze hung over the bay.

Harry felt the heat on his forehead. His mind was confused but his brain was racing.

Nardina was behind him now putting her hands around his waist.

"Harryee, I'm sorry but I cannot tell cos' I get murdered if I do". Nardi was not crying but she was shaking with fear.

Harry was angry. He was desperate to find out what had happened to Victor and Clive but the main reason for coming to Spain had been to sort out the deal, catch a bit of sun and flirt with the women. Murder and falling in love were not part of the deal.

"Nardi, you're goin' to have to be straight with me, or I'm off".

Harry was never one to mince his words.

"Harryee, don't leave me, don't leave me, promise!

"That depends Nardi".

The couple were hand in hand, standing close to the car. Nardi suggested they drive back to the hotel and she would tell him all she knew.

A small motor bike rushed past them. The young rider in black leathers handed Nardi a long envelope and dashed off. Harry tried in vain to catch the intruder but he sped off.

Nardina nervously opened the envelope. It was a short typewritten note. It read:

Don't say anything or you'll die.

It was unsigned.

Nardina was trembling. She feared every move she made.

Unknown to her Harry had noticed something about the rider. He had three fingers on his left hand. Also on his neck there was an unusual tattoo marked "CRU"?

"The CRU", thought Harry.

"What and who was on that bike? Harry's mind drifted to some far off place where coal dust once hung in the air and where beer cannot be sold in Euro.

～

Warlord was having his weekly trip to Coxburn, where the fish was fresh and the chips were made from real potatoes. He was a phenomenon in the village. He worked down the pit like many of his contemporaries. The excessive amount of coal dust was his excuse for the thirst he had acquired for beer.

But Warlord had a serious side. He always wanted fair play and one of his friends was out in Spain and another had gone out but was now in a morgue, where no one understood English.

Warlord thought that Harry was just being a bit of a playboy and that he was not interested in finding Victor's killer. He thought the sight of Victor's widow; Vicky would stir him up.

Warlord, Victor Plum, Trevor Pike, Pikey to his close friends and Harry had all been in the same class at school. He did not know Clive but was suspicious of anyone in a foreign territory. Spain was definitely foreign to Warlord.

The four men formed the CRU, the Coxburn Retail Union. It was questionable whether it was legitimate and no one knew if it existed. It did exist but it was clandestine.

Sending consignments of alcohol and tobacco from Spain and selling it on was one thing but how did Victor get murdered pondered

Warlord. Perhaps Vicky might find out. Victor was the financial wizard. He was the one who kept the books in order, Warlord was the 'Trojan horse' and nobody got by him. Harry was the negotiator.

There were also associates, gofers like Pikey and a friend, Jack Flashman. They had both worked down the pits in Durham. Both were in a different underworld now. No coal dust or white finger but liable to get their fingers burnt more often than they did a shift at the pit.

Pikey and Flashman were as ruthless as their former working environment. On the surface, bags of humour. Cold, dreary and manipulative on the inside. The two men were always keen on a bit of the action!

Neither Pikey nor Flashman liked Victor Plumtree. They also discarded Harry Farmer, seeing him as a bit of a comic. They saw the surface but did not understand the interior. They were the perfect pair for an execution.

No one would suspect and there would be no questions. But two men who had spent most of their lives down the pit and since then propping up the bar of the local workmen's club were unlikely assassins abroad. Doing a job in Newcastle or Middlesbrough might be their forte, but the Costa del Sol?

Just as their appearance deceived so to did their connections. Both men were approaching their sixties, but they had sons who had knuckles to bear, where brain power exercised little but frustration. They had no scruples!

In a taxi, on a plane, into a hotel, execution carried out and jobs done!

Built like two concrete posts more often seen holding motorway bridges, 'Bummer' Brian and 'Grinder' Gary had seen more of a Malaga bar life than the scenery of the Mediterranean but they had learnt more about the seedy underworld of the territory.

Costa dell Sol had no fear to them, the same scenery and low life in a tacky disguise!

Bumping off Plumtree and some ex-patriot, making it in sunny Spain held no emotion, just instant gratification.

Around the pubs and clubs of the north east of England they were fearless and were to be feared. A number of stretches in prison, for GBH and armed robbery, they handled themselves as a team.

~

Harry's relationship with Nardina was getting too serious. Harry had been married once and he was cautious of the commitment. He was smitten by Nardina and her dark Mediterranean features but apart from their casual relationship he did not want anything more than that at present.

Nardina felt vulnerable and Harry knew that it would be easy to submit to her demands and the financial security she provided.

As he lay next to Nardina, the morning breeze crept through the open patio. Harry could not remember it been left open. But last night the mixture of vodka, red wine and wild passion numbed reality.

They had one thing in common; both of them were living in a fish bowl. Clive and Victor were dead. There were no explanations and Victor's body had been removed from his bedroom. His best friend, Warlord had not been in contact for a couple of days and then there was the intruder. The Spanish Police did not have any leads on how Clive met his death and there was no active investigation.

Harry felt trapped. He liked to be in control. Freedom and independence were Harry's hallmarks. In a squeeze Harry aimed for the tight corner of light.

While not abandoning Nardina, he felt constrained. They could not go off somewhere for the moment, at least.

After a weekend of intense passion, Nardina awoke and she was aware of Harry's pre-occupation. She turned to him and they kissed tenderly.

"Harryee, I worry about you. You are tense". Nardina was rubbing Harry's neck and shoulders, in an attempt to relax him. But Harry's mind was miles away!

Harry rang Warlord on his mobile. There was no reply.

The days that followed were arduous for Harry, not in a physical sense but mentally they were torture.

Nardina tried in vain to comfort Harry but even their lovemaking lacked the sparkle. Harry was depressed and this was unlike him.

His mind resembled a spider weaving a web.

It was Tuesday morning and Harry had not slept well. Tossing and turning, all night, he crept out of bed and made a coffee. Tasting the first sip Harry heard his mobile ringing by the bed. He answered with anticipation. It was Warlord.

"Harry, I think I know who fucking things up". Warlord was not generous with words. His crude style was not intended to offend.

"What do ya mean Worrie, you know? …."   Harry's spirit sprung to life.

"Do you remember, Pikey and Flashman, I think they have got their two lads exercising their knuckles Harry". Harry knew that Pikey and Flashman had little brainpower but liked to upset things.

"Where are the two blockheads Dave?"

Warlord did not answer immediately.

"I think they are out where you are Harry mate!". Harry felt a mixture of elation and anxiety.

"Are ya alright Harry", Warlord's words were genuine and lingering.

"Speak to ya soon Worrie, don't worry", Harry meant to be reassuring.

"Make sure ya do, I know what ya like, ya bast…

Warlord's phone went dead, no signal.

~

Knowing whom the intruders were was one thing; Harry wasn't sure what would happen next.

Harry went for a walk. He didn't know that Vicky had booked into the 'Rio Grande'.

Walking along the corridor to reception he heard a broad and loud Durham dialect.

"Harry, what ya doing here bonnie lad". Harry looked around thinking that a Geordie accent in Benalmedina was something of a rarity.

Vicky was an attractive woman in her late thirties. She had gained some weight in recent years. Her accent was as broad as her hips. She was all women but had the temper and fist power of a man.

Harry had met Vicky several times but it was Victor he knew well.

"Catchin a bit of sun before I go back, Vicky?". Harry looked over to Vicky, who was wearing cheap sunglasses.

"Aye, it's freezin' back home, so I'm goin' to make the most of it". There was something insincere about Vicky, thought Harry.

There was little to attract Harry to Vicky. She was very overweight and her appearance was tacky. He was a little surprised by her emotional distance. After all, Victor had been dead for a matter of weeks.

Harry felt a gentle breeze as he left the hotel entrance. The air was not as humid and the cool interlude was pleasant. He fancied a walk down into Benalmedina. It was late morning and the town was about half a mile from the hotel. There was a row of shops down both sides of the twisting terrace, with bars averaging one in three shops.

A cool pint of beer was the just the ticket thought Harry as he entered one of the many British pubs. The pub was dark but cool. The Kronenbourg had a kick to it!

The pub was not crowded. The barman, Mike was from Manchester and there was an array of Manchester City

Football Club memorabilia cluttered around the small bar. The talk was about sport and there was an English Premiership match on the TV screen. Newcastle United were playing Manchester United. The rain was driving down on the pitch.

Outside in the narrow street there was excitement brewing. A crowd had amassed around what appeared to be two bald-headed youths scrapping it out like primitive animals. Kicking, punching and head butting.

First impressions were of the British yob who infiltrate Spanish bars. Harry thought he recognized one of the pair. One was Trevor Pike's son. The other, as he got closer to the action was an unknown. As edged Harry edged forward to the baying crowd, he felt something hard and cold at the back of his head. He swung around, ducked and hit hard at the heavy flubber that gazed at him. Flashman looked hard at him.

'Grinder' Pike was still involved in the fray. 'Bummer' Flashman was keen to finish Harry off. But Harry's leaner frame propelled strength and power that Bummer underestimated.

As well as his physical and mental agility Harry had mastered skills in martial arts and combat. Bummer didn't know what to expect. Brawling in bars was his only experience.

Harry gave a clear warning to Bummer but didn't wait for his reply before landing a shot that winded him. Bummer had a heavy build but hadn't seen a gym for years. Chips, endless amounts of curry and lager was his regular diet.

Grinder's brawl was less captivating to the crowd and they turned their attention to Harry's execution of Bummer. It wasn't pretty, but there was a sense of excitement.

The local Policia had been alerted but turned a blind eye and they decided to have coffee in a nearby café keeping an eye on the main event. Grinder and Flashman were irritants they were keen to see them off their patch.

Harry succeeded in seeing Flashman off. Bruised, bleeding and bumbling, Bummer limped off to the taunts of the crowd. Harry was their hero!

Grinder had disappeared, his ego dented and without Bummer. He was part of a double act, not an individual performer.

Harry made his way back into the bar. It was time for iced vodka!

Chapter 3
Casting the Net

The brawl in the street and the hangover it generated caused Harry more anguish. He had slept well but the thumping headache had more to do with unanswered questions than the volume of vodka consumed into the early hours.

Nardina brought him coffee. Harry looked at her slightly dazed wondering why he had stayed with one woman. He often tired of the same woman. Harry didn't like commitment.

Who was really out to get Harry?

Harry pondered his next move. As Harry's mind went into overdrive, his mobile phone rang.

"Harry mate". Warlord's voice was monotone.

"You still alive then?" Warlord was serious.

"So what have you heard Worrie?" Harry was in pensive mood

"Flashman and Pikey's lads nearly had you Harry, you gonna have to watch yer' self mate". The warning from Warlord had a sinister ring to it.

"Dave, who's after me then. You know don't ya?"

"Harry you're a wanted man mate and the talk in the club is that you killed Victor and the other guy. It doesn't matter what I say…" Harry felt for the first time that his friendship with Dave Warlord was under threat.

For a few seconds Harry collected his thoughts. Then he retorted.

"Dave, what do you think, forget about everybody else. Me and you have been mates for a long time….". Harry's words seemed to sink into an abyss. Warlord was gone. Was it a lost signal or something more sinister?

Harry's relationship with Nardina was suffering. His mind was pre-occupied. He was edgy and arguments between them were a regular event. There was still chemistry between them but Harry didn't want to give Nardina the wrong impression. At the moment he needed fun. Nardina was looking for a permanent lover. They were looking for different things.

The last phone call from Warlord haunted Harry. He came to Spain to sort out a deal for the CRU. Now he was in the frame for a murder he didn't commit.

~

The lorry heading for the Freight Depot at Alicante Airport was pristine. A Volvo Streamliner. It shone in the night-lights but there was nothing conspicuous about it's cargo. After all Hargreaves and Palmer were legitimate import and export carriers registered in Spain. Robin Hargreaves was the 'front man'. Harry was the so-called 'silent' partner.

Robin was the same age as Harry, lean and athletic, but also a reformed alcoholic. Whatever the consignments Robin looked upon them as items of profit. He was ruthless and not to be taken for granted. As a younger man in the Army he was a light - weight boxer. To customers and clients he was quite sophisticated but in his peer group he was foul mouthed and lacked tolerance. He had many a spat with the CRU, he liked Harry and his association with Warlord, Plumtree, Flashman and Pike was strictly business.

Unknown to Victor Plumtree, Robin was having an affair with Vicky. It was very much convenience rather than affection or sexual attraction. Vicky got a great deal of esteem but her free tongue gave Robin all of the information he needed on the Coxburn Retail Union.

~

Harry hadn't heard anything from Warlord in over a week. He wondered what was wrong and if Dave was all right. For a few minutes he thought about a return to Coxburn. He then dismissed the idea, pondering on Warlord's words when they last spoke on the phone. Normally, going back to Durham would result in a warm welcome but there would be no red carpet waiting for him.

~

A heavy cloud of smoke hung over the semi-circular bar of Coxburn Workingmen's Club. The club was the hub of village life. Some villagers would call it an institution. Others would whimsically suggest that many of the punters should be in one.

Warlord was sipping on a pint of John Smith's Bitter. His face showed signs of strain. Flashman and Pikey were chuckling at the end of the bar, much to his annoyance.

The bar was not full but the early evening drinkers were arriving. The Blackstone boys, Bobby Purvis and a couple of itinerant customers.

Dilys Robinson had worked as a barmaid for as long as anyone could remember and Kevin Robson, the steward was the coolest and one of most liked and trusted people around.

Dilys had a tongue that could sting.

"When's this bloody booze comin' over from Spain", grunted Flashman.

"Is Harry still alive Worrie? Flashman was teasing Warlord but he didn't respond. He continued to gaze at his beer and inhaled hard on a cigarette.

Warlord had never left the village he grew up in. He despised hot and clammy weather. Spain was not just foreign to Warlord. It was unthinkable to leave the Northeast, even though by air Spain was a little over two hours away.

Suddenly, Warlord came out of the daze that was depressing him and unleashed a verbal barrage that echoed around the large room.

"I'm bloody pleased we're not relying on you two for results. Harry's out there doin' his bit and all you and Pikey can do is get drunk and complain".

Give the lad some credit. It was not often that Warlord exploded but when he did you could feel the tremors.

Dilys took up the cudgel and laced into Flashman and Pikey.

"You two couldn't be straight if you lay down in a line". Dilys was stoking up for an argument.

Flashman and Pikey were aghast at Dilys' outburst. Women did not perturb them usually but Dilys was different. She could give as much as she got and they secretly respected her.

Dilys, despite her bluntness could be trusted. She was fiercely loyal to Warlord and to Harry Farmer.

"Where is Harry exactly, Worrie?" There was genuine concern in her voice.

"A place called Benalmedina". Warlord motioned towards Flashman and Pikey.

"Them two know where, cos their two blockhead sons tried to carve him up".

Warlord was shaking with anger, his face had gone scarlet with rage.

"We're not listening to this rubbish" raged Flashman.

"We're off" blurted Pikey, who was always in the shadows of Flashman.

"You've always been off, you two. Just like mouldy cheese!" Laughter rang around the bar but Flashman and Pikey were grim-faced.

Kevin remained quiet and listened. There were times to keep your mouth shut and this was an occasion.

Warlord ignited the flame with his outburst. Now there was a bush fire!

Flashman and Pikey shouldn't have been surprised by the popularity enjoyed by Warlord. He had a lot of power and control. They were by comparison a couple of jellyfish. Creeping out of the inferno they were like two scolded schoolboys. Their macho status was dented. Subdued anger was not something they were comfortable with.

Their response to feelings was normally immediate and irrational. They would seek retribution.

~

Harry was making the most of the last few days in Benalmedina. He decided that he needed to move on. Not back to Durham but to another Mediterranean venue.

Greece was one of Harry's favourite places. He planned the next few days and the tearful goodbye with Nardina. Harry would miss her but sentiment was not big on his list of priorities.

Harry rang Robin. He felt that as his loyalties in Durham were unclear at present, Robin was an ally, even if it was a business acquaintance. He wanted to check out his allegances.

Robin was at home in his plush villa, up on the hill overlooking the harbour. It was an ideal location. Surrounded by cypress trees and detached from neighbours, it provided a retreat for Robin.

It was difficult to penetrate the security that surrounded Robin. He was determined to protect his privacy and also his business interests.

Robin and Harry met when they were both in the Army. They had been in many scuffles and close shaves in Northern Ireland, the Falklands and Bosnia. Now as business associates their assignments provided different risks. The two men shared much in combat but their backgrounds contrasted greatly.

While Harry was loyal to his Durham roots, Robin had dismissed his east London upbringing and rarely returned to the UK. Harry and Robin had a pact: personal life should be kept personal but business was something important to both of them. No secrets, double-crossing or side deals!

Robin had been to Coxburn before with Harry. He met Warlord, Plumtree, Flashman and Pike. He had always fancied Vicky. Plumtree's widow and they have had regular romps. There is little in the relationship but sexual pleasure and pillow talk is often about Vicky informing on the CRU.

Both Harry and Robin are angry at the CRU.

"Heard anything from Warlord Harry?" Robin poured out Harry a generous vodka in a tall glass half filled with ice.

The two men sat opposite each other on matching leather sofas. A long glass coffee table was positioned between them.

"Nothin mate. They're playing silly buggers!" Harry was sipping his vodka. He was in a determined mood.

"I was thinking about goin over there but…" Robin interrupted his associate.

"Not a good idea Harry. I'll go instead, it's less risky". Harry thought hard on Robin's suggestion. He considered the merits but didn't like to miss out on the action.

"Listen mate, I know what you're like but leave it to me, I'll sort the gits out!" Robin poured two more vodkas and the two men settled down to a long drinking session.

"Robin, any action around here?" Harry knew that Robin always had women around him. No serious relationships, that suited Harry at present. He was trying to get Nardina out of his head.

"Yeah, I'm seeing this babe, Sinita and she has a friend. Two blonde Spanish flirts, just like us". The two men were laughing.

Harry's relationship with Nardina had been something of a holiday romance. But they had drifted into an emotional tide.

Clive's death, Nardina's feelings of rejection and a chemistry that developed were not a foundation for a permanent relationship. Even if it was, Harry didn't want that. He desperately wanted answers to the deaths of Clive and also Victor Plumtree.

Harry didn't want to break their relationship totally. He would keep in touch and keep their relationship casual. But he was no one- woman man. He liked to play the field.

Robin and Harry had consumed a full bottle of vodka and as they contemplated some food, there was a ring at the doorbell. It was Sinita. Clad in a skimp floral dress, she wore little make-up apart from deep pink lipstick. She had long slim legs and a trim figure.

Harry noticed the close eye contact between Robin and Sinita. Sinita's friend Amelia looked like her 'twin'. Identical dress and a facial similarity that was uncanny.

Harry knew the score. There would be no great introductions. It was obvious to Harry that the two girls were hookers. He felt frisky and the leggy blonde would excite him for a while.

Robin's house was huge and there were six bedrooms in all. The two couples went off for an afternoon of lustful passion.

~

Harry woke up; the late afternoon sunshine was streaming though the wide window. His itinerant lover had left. He could hear the moans of sexual satisfaction from the adjoining bedroom. Harry felt hungry but decided to leave a note for Robin. He headed away from the villa into the town and one of the many cafes.

There was a small place close to the 'Rio Grande'. As he approached the entrance, two men he had seen before confronted him. Young Flashman and Pike shaded the sunlight and Harry's attempt to enter the café.

"What's your game lads?" Harry's eyes were fixed on the two men.

"The CRU want to see you Harry and we are going with you!" Flashman and Pike were solid, their manner was uncompromising.

"I see, how should I trust you two then?" Harry continued to stare at them, unmoved by their physical presence.

"When this going to happen then?" Harry's mind was clear. A return to Durham didn't frighten him.

"There's a flight back to Newcastle at 5.30 this afternoon. We'll meet you back here at 3 okay Harry, don't cross us!" Harry shrugged his shoulders, placing his arms out in front of him.

"Okay lads, I'll be here". The two heavyweights looked bewildered. They expected a struggle.

Harry had an intelligent mind. Flashman and Pike used their brawn. They acted on an impulse.

After breakfast of bacon and eggs, Harry decided to go and see Nardina. They had not seen each other for a few days.

Nardina was predictable in a number of ways. She was always at the 'Rio Grande'. Apart from visiting her sick mother in a nearby hospital, Nardina's movements were not difficult to trace.

Harry found that Nardina had not been seen since the previous day. She had gone off to see her mother in the afternoon but had not been seen since. The ever helpful and trusted Sanchez was behind the bar and had served Harry an iced vodka.

Sanchez looked cleaner and less intoxicated than usual. He could speak English and had a limited English vocabulary.

He could hold a conversation and liked sport, particularly his hometown club Barcelona.

"Harryee, I think Newcastle will get a beating in the Champions League at the Neu Camp on Thursday.

Harry was keen on football but was more interested in the whereabouts of Nardina. Sanchez seemed clueless as to her whereabouts.

"We'll see Sanch." Harry didn't want to engage in a lengthy conversation, not today anyway.

Harry wandered off and headed for his room to pack some clothes. He called at Nardina's apartment; he had a key but knocked at the door. Nardina was not there and there were no signs of anything suspicious. Everything in the apartment was neat and tidy.

It was 1.30 in the afternoon. In a little under two hours he would be heading for the airport with the two morons. He would be having a drink with Warlord in Coxburn Club at 8 o'clock. That was the plan!

Perhaps Nardina had gone off to some relative or an acquaintance, perhaps another boyfriend. Harry was trying to be rational but deep down he was very worried about his lover.

Sitting outside on the terrace, he wondered where she was but he was at a loss to know where to find her.

Harry had to get ready for the 5.30 flight. He pondered on the prospect of spending the next few hours with the two morons.

As Harry left the hotel with a small bag, he felt that the two weeks presented more questions than answers. Would there be any solutions in Durham?

~

Flashman and Pike's 'off shoots' were in the 'Pelican' bar drinking pints of lager. At first they ignored Harry. He wasn't bothered. He wouldn't choose these two social misfits to have a drink with. Harry ordered his customary vodka.

Harry thought hard about going back to Coxburn. He had not told Robin and Warlord did not know of his visit. The two blockheads were under orders from somebody. Soon he would be back in the hub of the village, the lounge bar and with his mate Warlord.

Flashman and Pike were asleep most of the journey. Harry was not in the mood for sleep. He had a sandwich and coffee. He would keep his mind clear for the many questions he and Warlord had for each other. The blockheads were meant to be his escorts but if Harry had chosen to stay in Benalmedina, these two would not stop him.

Chapter 4
Stirring Passions

The two women were sipping cocktails in a shaded area of the beach. They had different backgrounds and accents but shared a common desire.

Vicky Plumtree had met Nardina on a number of occasions. Vicky had visited Nardina and Clive at the 'Rio Grande'. She had a stormy relationship with Victor and at times would get a cheap flight to Malaga.

Victor presented as decent and hard working but when in drink he was fiery. He was used to controlling finance and the CRU was something more than an interest. Vicky was fed up with the antics of Flashman and Pike and put up with Warlord for the sake of Victor.

Vicky knew of Harry but just as a friend of Victor and Warlord and someone who knew Robin. She fancied Robin more than he did her.

It was very much living for the moment for the two women. They were independent women and financially they could do as they please.

Nardina loved Harry and she missed him a lot. He was there for her when she needed him most, feeling vulnerable after Clive's death. Deep down she hoped their relationship could be rekindled.

～

Harry and the two blockheads got into a taxi at Newcastle Airport. They said little to each other during the half-hour journey to Coxburn.

Harry allowed Flashman and Pike to sit on either side of him, not because he feared them but to ridicule them. They looked so foolish.

The atmosphere in the club sensed anticipation. Harry's return. Harry was a popular guy with many.

There was the usual predictability, routines, same faces and wise cracks ringing around the lounge bar.

Warlord stood at the bar. He had been told by Flashman that 'the boys' were bringing Harry back like a captive.

Flashman and Pike were gloating. Achievement was something that was alien to them. They were to be pitied and their two off springs resembled two walking time bombs!

Warlord was a good listener, but there was a limit to how much he could take from these two.

"What time's the prisoner coming then?". Warlord looked across at Flashman, goading him but Flashman was not in the mood for jokes. He rarely laughed.

Flashman, felt important. Bummer and Grinder had brought Harry back.

"Should be back anytime now Worrie".

Like a hero Harry entered the room.

"Alright lads". Harry was relaxed and back with the people he knew and had grown up with.

There was drama but not the reception Flashman or Pike would have wanted.

61

"What's been happening then?" Harry's eyes focussed on Warlord.

"I bet there's a few around here, who thought I was dead".

"Or wished I was dead, eh Jack". Harry was feeding off the good vibes around the room.

Amid the laughter, there were a few silent glances. The Blackstone boys, Gerry and Trevor looked on. Bob Snow, a colourful character, whose wit endeared him to many in the club hummed a tune and shouted to Harry.

"Come over here man and have a drink". Bob was sincere and wanted to cut the tension that had developed.

Warlord was silent and Harry wondered what was up. He had been looking forward to meeting Worrie but they seemed to be in a 'stand-off'. Just like two boxers in the ring, waiting for the pre-match euphoria to subside.

Bob's intervention was as timely as the many songs he played on the organ as an entertainer some years ago.

Harry hugged Bob's rounded frame and the two laughed loudly.

"It's good to see ya Bob, I've got some cigars for you... you're favourites!

"That's great Harry, I've been worried about ya lad"

"We all have", chirped Dilys, who was serving behind the bar.

"This bloody lot need sorting out. Jack Flashman and Trevor Pike think they own the place".

Warlord moved towards Harry and Bob Snow.

"Harry we need to talk". Warlord was somber.

"Okay Worrie, no problem mate". The two men were eye to eye.

"Alone Harry, just me and you". Harry detected mistrust in Warlord's voice.

Warlord trusted few people, even his closest friends and Harry had been up until now a special pal.

To run the Coxburn Retail Union Warlord adopted a ruthless style. He knew that Flashman and Pike had been keen to muscle in and he was determined not to lose his grip. Losing Plumtree had been a blow to Warlord. Victor was a wizard with money and this was foreign territory to Warlord. He could handle the brawn but not the banks. They were the perfect foil, Chairman and Treasurer of the club - their official titles concealing the conspiracy.

Coxburn Workingmen's Club and Institute was the name above the door. It was a fairly typical club; successful and heaving with characters as buoyant as the bank balance.

Most villages and communities would promote those characteristics that make it different. For some it is about being the 'Village in Bloom' and for others it might be some piece of the landscape. A stream or discarded railway track, dating back to the industrial vibrancy of the area and region. All villages have some significant spot that represents its nerve centre. Coxburn's nerve centre was the club.a perfect foil for its illicit or more secretive enterprises.

Warlord had fought hard all of his life and had no intention of anyone getting the better of him, even Harry Palmer. He liked Harry but at times his attitude worried him. Warlord was not 'laid back'.

The two men went into an office normally occupied by the Club Secretary. Neither sat down.

"What the hell's goin' on Worrie?"

"You seem to have the world on ya shoulders man".

"Harry, they reckon you killed Victor and you know how I feel about that"

Warlord clenched his teeth and his face turned crimson.

"But Worrie, I wouldn't and couldn't have done that. I liked Victor, even though he was a funny bugger at times". Harry looked for a reaction from Warlord.

Warlord was about to speak when the door burst open.

Flashman and Pike sensed it was their moment. They were heading for Harry. But it was Flashman who made for Harry with an opening punch.

Warlord exploded, in a way Harry had not seen before.

"Will you two get out, I am sorting things out here. I don't need you. You're comedians!"

Harry beat off Flashman's cuff and pushed Pike aside. He was the lightweight and Harry had to exert little effort.

Warlord let fly at both men and it was clear he was out to kill them both. Kicks and punches were landing at Flashman's head and rolling belly. Pike retreated like a scorned cat. He was the coward who fired the bullets for Flashman!

Harry wanted to finish the two of them off but Warlord saw this as his fight.

"Keep out of this Harry, I want to talk to you when this lot have gone". Warlord was in control.

~

Robin Hargreaves had been trying to ring Harry most of the morning but he sensed his business partner had gone. He wondered whether he was all right but then pondered about their transactions. Who was in control at the CRU?

He'd arranged to meet Vicky Plumtree for lunch but he didn't expect her to be with Nardina. He planned on lunch and then an afternoon soirée but when he saw the slim dark Mediterranean beauty he became infatuated.

It was not the low cut bright red dress that left little to the imagination but her stunning looks that made it obvious to Vicky where Harry's eyes and mind were.

Vicky kissed Robin with an eagerness that sought to dispel his attentions for Nardina.

"Robin, darlin' this is Nardina, a friend of mine. She's been having it rough lately and so I invited her along. Is that okay?" Robin was not complaining. In fact it was obvious to Robin that it was Vicky and not Nardina who was having it rough.

Vicky explained how she and Nardina had met some years ago and when Clive was alive she would stay with the couple at their hotel. Robin listened but his eyes were transfixed on Nardina. She had barely spoken, part from acknowledging Robin.

"What do you do Robin?" Nardina interrupted Vicky in full flow.

"A bit of this and that". Robin's guard was up, at least on the subject of his business activities.

"Vicky tells me yur a friend of Harryee Farmer!" Robin was frank in his reply.

"Yeah I know him, but are you..." Vicky refused to be ignored and was ranting on about Victor's will.

"Victor's going home tomorrow. They're releasing his body from the morgue. His funeral is on Saturday". Vicky began to cry momentarily. There was something false about her distress. Bold attention seeking Robin thought.

Robin smiled sympathetically but then turned his attention to Nardina. He didn't mention Clive but was keen to know if she was involved with anyone.

"So you're running the hotel on your own now Nardina, that must be difficult for you?" Robin was discreet and Vicky did not sense more than a passing interest.

"Yes, si, I know the business and Clive he was away a lot. I have staff but I like to know what's goin on". Nardina was controlled and Robin was impressed.

"Harryee was good to me when Clive died". Robin detected that Nardina felt something for Harry and he was envious.

Nardina began to cry and Robin was taken aback. Only minutes ago she had been quite resolute, unaffected it seemed by Clive's death.

"When did you last see Harryee Nardina?" Robin was keen to know Harry's whereabouts.

"He went off three days ago, said he was seeing a friend but I've not heard from him since.

Vicky had grown impatient and gone through to Robin's kitchen to make some sandwiches. There was chilled champagne and melon in the fridge.

Robin liked the good things, just like Harry, which is why they were compatible in many ways.

Nardina did not show the same interest in Robin as he did for her. It was obvious to him that despite making more than a pass at her she was very fond of his business partner.

"Let's eat". Vicky brought through a tray of sandwiches.

"I've left the champagne in the kitchen. Go and get it would you Harry darling". Vicky's overacting was irritating Robin.

"Okay, two minutes". Robin went to get the bubbly and Vicky followed him.

"What the hell's goin on Robin. You're all over in a rash with her. I want your attention, please". Vicky was up close and teasing Robin about their afternoon activities.

"I was just being sociable, that's all. She is your friend, isn't she?" Robin and Vicky kissed like lovers.

After lunch Nardina made an exit and returned to the 'Rio Grande'. There was something determined about her manner.

～

Harry and Warlord sat crouched. A bottle of malt whiskey was on the table and half consumed. It was not Harry's style. Vodka was his preferred liquor but Warlord was calling the shots.

"Listen Harry, I want you tell me what happened when you got over to Spain, where was Victor?" Warlord's interrogation skills were not the best Harry thought.

Harry explained in great detail his movements from leaving Newcastle, arriving at the Rio Grande and how he found Victor's body in the shower cubicle of his room.

" How the hell then, did Victor get into your room?" Warlord wanted answers.

"Worrie, I don't bloody know. I'd just arrived. Victor was in there when I put the key in the door". Harry was patient but it was wearing thin

"What about this Spanish hussy Clive's missus?" Warlord was unrelenting in his questioning.

"How do ya know her Worrie". Harry sensed he had Warlord on the ropes.

"I know of her, Victor mentioned her sometime I think". Warlord was a little winded by Harry's quick exchange of words.

Harry was a little wary of Warlord. Did he have some part in Victor's death and was he trying to put him in the frame?

~

Nardina was attending some private papers. The mahogany bureau was cluttered with letters and bills belonging to Clive. She had ignored them for weeks. Much of the correspondence was mundane.

Unpaid fees. Clive had a share in the yacht and there were bills for maintenance.

There was one letter that caught Nardina's eye. Unopened, it was handwritten and had a sweet scent. Nardina thought the perfume was familiar, like the one she uses – a 'Givenchy'.

Her heart had stopped aching for Clive. As she read the letter it became obvious that Clive had a mistress but also a 'love child'. Francesca, the child's mother was quite forceful in her letter, pouring out love to Clive but wanting it at a financial price.

Clive's fishing trips were clearly a front. Now as Clive's widow, the prospect of lengthy litigation loomed.

Nardina had worked hard with Clive to build the business. She was loathe to give up a chunk of this all for the sake of Clive's indiscretions. Nardina needed someone to talk to, yes a lawyer at some point but where was Harry, she thought?

~

Harry and Warlord had drunk a lot and their conversation was a muddle of words. They argued and laughed, but most of all they fried their brains!

The two men had stopped arguing and indeed anything else for that matter. They were hugging together but it was difficult to determine whether this was renewed friendship or incapacity.

Dilys came into the office and found the two men slumped. A bottle and a half of malt whiskey consumed. She brought them black coffee but she wondered if the caffeine would do the trick, or would something more drastic be necessary.

"Worrie, Harry, come on. Sort yourselves out. It's chucking out time downstairs. There was some moaning but little sign of the two men coming to, let alone standing up.

The constant sound of Dilys demands had the effect and both men finally came around. They settled for something to eat at a local pizza shop and a walk back to Worrie's place.

"Harry, you're not leading me on about Victor are you. You never killed him did you, cos' I know what Victor could be like. His was a bugger about money!"

"Worrie, there are people who could drive me but poor old Victor is not one of them. Mind you, I don't trust Vicky".

"Neither do I, Harry. She's a scheming bitch that one".

The two pals settled for pepperoni and garlic bread. There was snooker on the TV and some cans in the fridge. They caught up on what had been happening, apart from Victor's death.

Warlord's two bedroomed flat was quite sparse but clean. Harry despite the sore head woke quite early. His clothes were all over the floor but could hear his mobile ringing.

It was Nardina; she was crying and quite agitated.

"Harry where are you, I need you please". Harry was usually cautious about women who turned on the emotional threats but he was quite fond of Nardina.

"Where did you go Nardi, you had gone when I came over to see you on Monday".

"I spent some time with Vicky Harry. You left me and I was lonely". Harry did not want the pressure but felt a little guilty.

He explained to Nardi about Bummer and Grinder and his trip to Durham.

"When can I see you Harry? Harry was not sure when he would return. He'd stay for Victor's funeral on Saturday.

"I don't know Nardi, I've got some business over here. I'll ring you later".

"Please do Harry, promise me darling". Harry was besotted by Nardina's voice.

"I will Nardi, promise. Take care".

"Harry I am getting some pressure and need to talk to you don't let me down".

"I will, promise". Harry needed to get his head together. The hangover was one thing but women needed careful handling.

Breakfast could wait. Harry took a long walk around Coxburn, which had changed little from the place, he grew up in. As he walked over the fields towards the site of the old Hall, he recalled fond memories, scary moments and his initiation as a libido raging teenager.

There was a stillness in the air and a suspicion and mystery that Harry associated with events in Benalmedina. Could there be some conspiracy that extended far beyond the CRU?

~

Vicky had boarded the 11.30 flight from Malaga bound for Newcastle. She was heading home to bury her husband. Robin had offered to travel with her, but Vicky declined. There was an expectation of a grieving widow and a boyfriend on her arm would not go down well.

Nardina had also wanted to come over with Vicky but her presence might provoke suspicion, or at least too many questions. Vicky wanted to soak up the sympathy of Coxburn folk where Victor had been such a popular figure. She wanted no complications.

Vicky's flight was delayed for two hours. This irritated her, as she was not comfortable in a foreign country. She rang Robin. She could hear voices in the background, women screaming and shouting. Robin was guarded.

"Hello Vicky, what's happening?" Vicky was agitated.

"Not a lot, where are you Robin? Robin was quick to answer.

"I'm in a bar with Harry, just business you know, that's where most of it happens!" Vicky was not amused. She knew where Harry was and did not being lied to.

Robin's phone remained on and she could hear a lot of intimate chat. Whatever business he was up to she didn't know, but she heard a muffled voice of a woman, who Robin referred to as Francesca.

Harry and Warlord met for a late breakfast of bacon and eggs in a local café. They talked about Victor's funeral the following day and plans for send off.

The club would play host after the funeral, where Victor's family and friends would drink, eat and drink, talking endlessly about a man that some, who would muscle in on the occasion didn't know or even liked. Anything for a meal ticket!

But what did Plumtree leave in his will. Jerome Chance, a local solicitor had worked for the CRU for a number of years. He was also Plumtree's solicitor. Warlord trusted Jerome, or at least he could manipulate him.

Jerome was not a bad manipulator either. His legal training taught him about being creative and finding loopholes even when they didn't exist. Just the man for the CRU!

The two men thought hard about complications. Flashman and pike were lying low; their egos were bruised.

"Vicky's as unpredictable as an unexploded bomb Harry". Warlord contemplated her return and mood.

"Worrie, don't worry. We can sort it out". Harry was confident but Warlord knew Vicky well and he was concerned.

Chapter 5
Deceptions and Dreams

Francesca was the woman Robin wanted Vicky to be. Like Vicky she was strong and ruthless but there the similarities ended.

Vicky lacked charm and tact. She opened her mouth at every opportunity, not thinking through the consequences. She flaunted but she was tacky.

Francesca was elegant by comparison, successful in business and more than satisfactory as a lover. They both had an appetite for success and Robin knew that she was out for all she could get. He could handle that!

He thought he saw a resemblance between Francesca and Nardina, not just in physical appearance but in their mannerisms.

~

Coxburn anticipated Victor Plumtree's funeral. It was a grey day, with rain clouds looming. The hot summer sun from the day before was replaced by clammy, still and expectant stormy weather.

Warlord had instructed Kevin Robson, the club steward to open the club at 10, an hour before Victor's funeral and there was a crowd gathering at 9.30. There was a strong drinking culture in the village.

The streets around the village were filled with cars. Saturday was a busy day in the village and there was a particular buzz around. It was as if a celebrity was getting a final send off but Plumtree was a celebrity of sorts.

Warlord, Flashman and Pike were standing at the bar like three stooges. Dressed in dark grey suits, black ties and white shirts, onlookers commented on their immaculate dress.

"They must have won the lottery or got a housekeeper apiece", chuckled Tom Wild, one of the oldest residents in the village. Tom knew every thing that was going on in Coxburn, who was doing what, where and with whom.

"Harry, you're a smart bugger today". Tom was always dressed in the same garb, a well-used cloth cap, tweed jacket and corduroys. Harry had settled for a black open neck shirt and dark Grey jacket. Not a man of convention! He had enough of that in the Army.

"Thanks Tom. I try".

"Look at those three over there. Remind me of those deputies when I was down the pit". Tom had a wry smile on his face.

Coal and quarries dominated the industrial and social image of the village. But there was more than dust in the air.

Anger, resentment and retribution fuelled the minds of Warlord, Flashman and Pike. But they were not united in whom they targeted.

Flashman and Pike resented the rejection and scorn from Warlord. For Warlord he wanted to eliminate the two irritants. They were bating for a fight.

❧

Nardina had received confirmation of Clive's estate. It was finalized and she was the sole beneficiary.

She so much wanted Harry to share her relief. Nardina missed Harry around. She decided to ring him.

Harry's phone rang out. He was heading out of the club with Dilys Robinson. They were walking in the direction of the village church. Harry answered his mobile.

"Harryee, when can I see you, I 'm missing you darling". Harry was keen to keep the conversation short.

"Listen Nardi, I am going to Victor's funeral. I can't talk right now. I'll ring you later". There was little emotion in Harry's voice and Nardina detected this.

"Harry please ring me later". The phone went dead.

~

Vicky was at the funeral parlor and insisted on the undertaker opening up the coffin. She wanted to see Victor's face for the last time and have a few moments with him on her own.

James Marriott, the undertaker warned her of body decomposition but as he lifted the lid he shared Vicky's anguish.

Victor's body was not in the coffin. Instead there was a consignment of blue labeled bottles of 'Absolute' vodka.

Vicky's screams could be heard outside the church.

"Where's my Vic?" She was hysterical, repeating his name over and over.

There was little James could do to placate her.

Vicky went running outside in the street. There was little her family or friends could do to stop her. Running towards a gathering crowd outside the church. Vicky was gunning for Harry Farmer.

"What the hell's goin' on. Some kind of joke eh!" Vicky was trembling with anger.

"I don't know what you're on about Vicky". Harry sensed a captive crowd, keen to know what was going on but also what drama would unfold.

"Bloody bottles of vodka in Vic's coffin". Vicky was struggling to contain herself.

Harry was mindful of Vicky's distress but was not inclined to comfort her.

There were some scuffles in the crowd. The Flashman and Pike boys had arrived. Some local youths still hung over from the previous night fancied flexing some muscles.

Warlord walked over to Harry and whispered in his ear.

"I see the consignment's arrived, but I didn't know we were trading in coffins Harry". Warlord was deadly serious.

Harry tried to reassure Warlord.

"Worrie I didn't know about this, honestly!"

Word got out to the crowd that Victor Plumtree's funeral could not take place. There was no body!

Harry had an idea. He would ring Robin and see if he knew anything. Robin had made arrangements for the consignment from Spain.

Robin's phone rang. There was no reply.

Harry made several calls to Robin and hated leaving messages. Eventually there was a response, the voice of a woman that sounded sexy and familiar.

She was panting.

"Robin's not here". She was quite abrupt.

"I'm Francesca".

"Where is he? Robin's voice was strong and eager.

"Don't know where he is".

"I'll get him to ring you, okay". Harry was convinced that Robin was with her and he was avoiding him.

Harry felt he was being cheated and this annoyed him. He thought for a few seconds and decided that he needed to go back to Spain. He needed to sort things out. Robin knew what was going on and making a fool of him.

There was chaos in Coxburn. This was no place for him. He needed to prove to the CRU that he was no soft touch!

Harry briefly returned to the club and had a few drinks with Warlord.

"I'm goin' over there Worrie". Harry had some steel in his voice.

Warlord sensed they were a team again.

"Keep in touch you bugger. I know what you're like with the women Harry".

"Don't worry, I'll find out where Victor's body is. Okay Worrie!

The two men shook hands. Harry phoned the airline for a standby ticket. He took a taxi to the airport and settled for coffee and sandwiches before boarding the flight.

Harry was tired but there was too much going on for him to sleep.

~

Robin was sipping cocktails in basking Mediterranean sun. He and his dark haired lover were out on the patio sunning themselves when the roar of a 4x4 took them by surprise.

Harry hired the Mitsibiushi Shogun from an Avis operator at the airport in Malaga.

He was confrontational and wasted no time with Robin. Harry caught him with a left hook.

This was not Harry's usual style. He was normally verbal but the words followed the punches.

"You two faced bastard". Harry was like a raging bull.

"What do you mean Harry?"

"Are you on something?"

"No, but you are into something Robin and we are supposed to be partners".

"Victor Plumtree, what happened to his bloody body."

Robin was motionless. The dark haired beauty was soaking a tissue to wipe away blood from his face. Robin's nose was gushing.

"I want some answers Robin. No one crosses me and that includes you".

Robin was able to speak but his words were slurred.

"Harry, I know nothing". There was something in Robin's response that sounded false.

Harry turned his attention to the woman. He gazed in to her eyes and felt he knew the face and eyes. Her tender body and mood reminded him of Nardina. But she didn't respond to him. He wondered if perhaps she had a twin?

The woman put out her hand.

"Can I get you a drink Harryee? She looked at him with apprehension.

"Yeah, give me vodka and ice". There was no calming voice.

Harry followed her into the kitchen. The woman walked like Nardina and Harry was convinced it was her.

"Hello Nardi". The woman looked at him, staring, but there was no soft or seductive voice.

"You mistake me for someone, I'm Francesca". Harry was not convinced. But he did feel chemistry developing.

Harry held her close. The perfume was Faberge. Before he knew it they were kissing passionately. Harry did not resist. Coxburn had been a celibate experience!

Robin was outside sleeping while Harry and Francesca romped in an upstairs bedroom. The afternoon sunshine was strong and the heat compared with the passionate temperature inside.

Harry's mobile rang. He didn't answer it. It was Warlord. But Harry had had little time to say to his friend. There had been no time to find out anything.

Francesca was a beautiful woman. She intrigued Harry. She was a woman of mystery!

Harry and Francesca left Robin's house after a shower and set off for dinner.

The sun had gone down a little and there were crowds gathering around the pubs and restaurants.

Harry and Francesca did not blend in with the romantic couples who huddled around the bar of 'The Don Juan'. Neither showed any emotion. Both were keen to find out more about one another.

Francesca's relationship with Robin was more about business than romance. They both used each other. Harry detected a cold and calculating mind and he revelled in a challenge.

Harry liked the fast lane and Francesca had a ruthless streak. He understood what attracted Robin to Francesca but what of their relationship. Other than sex what else did they have in common?

Francesca was not a woman to be bought over. Plying her with endless cocktails would only increase suspicion. He decided to have a carefree night but not to let his guard down.

Harry talked to Francesca about different business ventures, casual talk about what to buy and when - property, shares and other investments. He discovered that Francesca had been married and divorced twice and that taking financial risks was more of a turn on than a long-term relationship.

The couple ate seafood and steak and there was a pretense.

Harry let out little about himself. Army life taught him to be cautious and guarded

"Harry, how do you come to know Robin". Despite drinking a number of white Russians Francesca was alert and energetic.

"We knew each other when we were in the Army and we have done some business". Harry watched Francesca's gaze. He had been used to interrogation and she was moving into gear.

"So you're not close then?"

Harry didn't answer her.

"What about you and Robin?"

Francesca beamed a wide smile.

"We're not lovers, if that's what you mean.

Harry smiles, revealing a sense of relief but it was part of the game.

"What about business?" Harry wanted to close in.

"You want me to tell you about Victor Plumtree don't you?"

Harry was curious.

"You knew Victor, did you?

Francesca bated Harry.

"Yes, he came over with his wife once. They knew... Clive!"

"You knew Clive?" Harry sensed an early point in the battle of wits.

"Clive and Victor had something going. Some kind of import or export operation down in Gibraltar.

Harry caught Francesca's eyes. There was a seductive glance.

Francesca owned a villa in the village of Mijas, up in the Andalucian Mountains. It was secluded and mirrored her personality. It was pristine. There was sophistication and elegance.

Harry was keen to continue his interrogation before a night of passion.

Francesca was talking freely but was not revealing the information Harry wanted.

"So Victor and Clive were friends? Harry was sipping a vodka and ice. Francesca had decided to change into a revealing black negligee. She also drank vodka.

"I don't know about friends, but they had some business thing". Francesca had a near perfect command of English.

Harry went for the kill.

" What about you and Clive?" Francesca looked confused.

Harry was enjoying himself.

"I mean business deals. You like to dabble and he did by the sound of it".

Francesca smiled teasingly.

"Yeah and he even faked his own death".

Harry was shocked by the disclosure but didn't show any emotion.

"Clive's alive then?

"I don't know but he was". Francesca realized that she had let slip some crucial information and that Harry would seize on it.

The following morning was hazy and Harry's energy levels had been tested by Francesca's sexual drive. His mind was alert.

It was 8am. He pulled on a shirt and left Francesca sleeping. Harry decided on a walk.

Outside of Francesca's villa there were clusters of trees, olives and cypresses. Harry grabbed his mobile. It was time to report to Warlord.

~

Warlord had been drinking heavily the night before. Beer was the normal menu but he liked whisky chasers. The sound of the phone made him wince.

"Who the bloody hell is this".

"Sorry mate, its Harry. Got some news".

"You bugger Harry. Tried ringing you yesterday. Been with a woman I bet"!

"What's happened mate?

Warlord was struggling with his words. The hangover was biting in!

Harry explained about Victor and Clive's business deals and that Clive was still alive

"Doesn't explain where Victor's body is, does it Harry".

Harry knew he had to find out more and Francesca could be his source.

"What about Vicky?"

Warlord had confused his friend.

"Worrie, what are you on about?

"Vicky disappeared on Saturday after the 'cock up'. Not been seen since. She must be over there.

"Anybody else disappeared?"

"What about the two clowns".

Warlord laughed out loud.

"No chance. Them two got banged up on Saturday night. Got blathered and they were fighting anyone who got in their way".

"I told Jerome Chance not to represent them if he wants to be retained by the CRU".

"So there's nobody to upset things, apart from Vicky but I'm sure you can handle her".

"I don't fancy her Worrie!"

"Just charm her mate, you're good at that!"

~

Harry returned to the villa. Francesca was still in bed but awake. She was naked and was wildly.

"I don't like my lovers walking out on me Harryee". Francesca's voice was Latin and seductive.

"Just went for a walk, but I'm back now". He peeled off his shirt and lay next to her.

For two hours the lovers romped. Again Harry thought how similar Francesca and Nardina looked. It was a mystery.

Francesca had some business in town at the bank. Harry had to catch up on some sleep. Francesca left Harry in bed. They arranged to meet at 7pm for dinner.

Harry thought he would look up Robin. But it would not be a social call. As far as Harry was concerned he wanted out of the partnership.

He drove up to Robin's. There was a car in the drive. Robin's Chevrolet was not there. A black Volkswagen Passat was a car he did not recognize.

Maybe another of Robin's women, Harry thought.

The front door was wide open.

Harry shouted as he walked in the hallway.

"Robin, are you there? Harry's voice echoed but there was no reply.

Harry went from the lounge into the dining area and the large kitchen. He thought he heard voices coming from upstairs.

As he walked up the stairway, he saw the outline of a woman. Moving closer towards the master bedroom, a body leapt out in front of him.

"What are you doin' here?" Harry had a bead of sweat across his forehead and it was running down his cheeks.

The slim frame moved away from him, down the staircase and out of the house. Harry gave chase and got a glimpse of the woman. She ignored his glance and voice.

"Nardina what's wrong?" She drove off at speed; a shower of dust blew in his face as the car sped off.

Harry went back into the house and up to Robin's bedroom. There were clothes strewn all over the large double bed.

Robin lay naked. A single bullet hole through his forehead.

Catching his thoughts Harry made for his hire vehicle. He did not want to be implicated in the death of his business partner.

Harry needed a drink more than ever. Robin was dead. Nardina had something to do with his murder. He couldn't start to think about motive. He was overwhelmed. But he wondered about Nardina and Francesca and whether they were the same people.

Chapter 6
Chasing Shadows

Harry thought that having Vicky around could be an advantage. Finding Victor was a priority for both of them. His only reservation was that Vicky opened her mouth at the wrong time and could scupper an opportunity.

Harry was not that close to either Victor or Vicky but he felt he owed it to Warlord to find Victor's body. He was determined to get to the root of what he suspected was not only a seedy venture but also a dangerous one.

Living in the fast lane gave Harry a lift. He liked wheeling and dealing and looked for an opportunity for a more quiet life, sunning himself in the Mediterranean.

He had sufficient put away to have a comfortable life style but he wanted the big break.

Harry felt it was time to report back to Warlord. He pondered.

~

Harry rang Warlord. He was at the club. He could hear the voices of Tom Wild, Bob Snow and the Blackstone boys, Gary and Trevor.

"Is that Harry, Worrie". Their voices seemed in unison.

"Listen Harry. Vicky has been on the phone. I want you to help her".

"Tell Vicky to meet me at 10.30 in the morning at The Beachcomber Café".

"Can I gave her your phone number Harry?

"No Worrie. I will help Vicky but I want to keep her at a distance, okay",

"I understand Harry. I'll tell her to meet you".

~

Harry met Francesca at the Don Juan. He noticed that she was pre-occupied. She kissed Harry firmly on the lips but it was more a spontaneous gesture than an expression of feeling. Harry was not sure about Francesca. He found her attractive and could not ignore her.

"What's wrong Francie?" Harry looked into Francesca's eyes.

"Nothing Harry, just business". She glanced away, but Harry knew she was hiding something.

Harry looked for answers, searched for solutions and raised suspicion.

Clive was still alive somewhere. Victor's body had not been found, He suspected that there was a bigger picture and that Nardina or Francesca would be under pressure.

Harry didn't understand.

"Francie, tell me what's wrong?"

"Harry, just some double dealing and I got caught up in it".

"C'mon Francie. It's more than that.

Francesca held him close.

"Make love to me tonight". Francesca was vivacious but her sensual mood was a distraction.

Harry would not resist but he wanted some answers.

The two lovers made their way back to Francesca's house. The lights were on and the front door was wide open.

As they got closer, and into the house Francesca and Harry could see that there was little that had been disturbed. There was no burglary but the intrusion made Francesca feel vulnerable.

She held Harry close. They kissed and Harry expected tears but there was no distress. Francesca displayed anger.

"Harry. I know Robin is dead and I know who killed him. Nardina".

Harry's suspicions had been confirmed.

"How do you know all this Francie?".

"Clive is alive. He spoke to me today, told me that Nardina had stabbed Robin in the chest".

"I know Francie. I was there. But it was not a stabbing but a single shot that killed Robin".

Francesca was shaking with anger.

"Why didn't you tell me Harry?"

"I'll be honest with you Francie, I thought you might tell me".

Harry was angry too.

"No one is telling the truth around here. You've been avoiding my questions. Now I want some answers". Harry was pounding the floor.

"Harry you don't want to get in too deep with all this".

"I am in deep Francie and I don't intend giving up, All, those years in the Army taught me one thing – to be resilient".

"Like you, I take risks but killing is not part of the deal. I saw enough killing in the fields of Bosnia and the streets of Northern Ireland!

"Okay Harry. I'll tell you what's goin' on".

"Clive and Victor were into some investments. Dodgy dealing cut up some people - big people. Victor is not the straight man everyone thinks".

Harry noticed that Francesca was talking of Victor as if he was still alive.

"What about Nardina?". Harry looked at Francesca, his eyes focussed.

"Where does she come into this?"

There was a pause. Francesca went to pour vodka out for each of them.

"I was Clive's lover and we have a child. I tried all ways to get Clive to leave her."

"What do you know about Vicky?

"Vicky who, or you mean Victor's wife".

"Nothing much only that she used to sleep with Robin a lot. Telling tales!"

"Who killed Robin then?".

Francesca looked confused.

"I told you. Nardina. Too many questions Harry for tonight. Take me to bed darling".

As they kissed Harry whispered in Francesca's ear.

"Have you ever killed anybody?"

She tried to distract him by loosening the buttons on his shirt. Harry was determined.

"You killed Robin didn't you Francesca?"

"No Harry. Nardina is my ……..

"Sister perhaps?

"Clive made her. He despised Robin and believes Robin tried to kill him".

Harry was not convinced by Francesca's story.

$\sim$

He had not been back to the Rio Grande for weeks. Harry was unsure of how Nardina would respond, particularly after the events of the previous day. But apart from anything else Harry needed his clothes. He had left the hotel in a hurry to return to Coxburn. There had been no one around reception when he left and Nardina had disappeared.

The Rio Grande had seen better days. Originally a family home it was adapted as a hotel in the 1970's and renovated in the last 10 years.

Clive had been in the Army and during his career he had been based in Gibraltar. He met Nardina 10 years ago. She knew the hotel trade. He didn't but had some experience of working in pubs.

In the Army Clive, Robin and Harry were pretty close. They had been involved in a number of enterprises, most of them were legal, and some were borderline.

The three men had an understanding. Despite their individual business interests on leaving the Army, they agreed to keep in touch and look out for each other.

Harry recalled his first visits to the Rio Grande. At a time when Clive and Nardina were very much in love things were fresh and there was a good atmosphere around the place. In contrast, the hotel now was a remnant of the past. It lacked the popularity it once had. Even in the peak season there were vacancies at the 40-room hotel.

But Harry's visit was not a sentimental journey. It was fact-finding.

Harry arrived at reception. Sanchez predictably was at the bar. Two young receptionists caught Harry's eye.

"Signor, a long time I see you. How are you?

Harry didn't want casual conversation.

" I'm fine. Is Nardina about?"

"Nardina, she not here as much. She is away a lot. Calls in some times. He's not here today. Sorry!"

Sanchez was vague. Harry thought he was lying.

"I'll call back later". Harry's words were clipped.

~

Harry was frustrated. He hated being given the run around.

There had been weeks of dramatic events. In the many parts of the world Harry visited, he had not experienced the same frustration. It haunted him. This affected him; it was personal and intrusive.

He kept his appointment with Vicky at the Beachcomber, a small bar close to the harbour.

Vicky was sipping a coke when he arrived. He wasn't sure what to say to her. They weren't exactly close and their last encounter was frosty.

Harry ordered a black coffee and joined Vicky.

"I was talking to Worrie last night Vicky. Did he speak to you?"

"Yes Harry. Listen, I know what you said to Worrie. Thanks"

Vicky seemed genuine.

"Have you heard anything about Victor Harry".

"No Vicky, nothing".

Vicky didn't know about Nardina and Robin's death. She agreed with Harry that there was an amazing resemblance between Nardina and Francesca.

"Vicky have you seen Nardina recently?"

"I saw her last week. She was up at Robin's house. When I arrived they had been arguing. I couldn't understand what she was doing there".

Vicky's account sounded plausible.

"Do you know where Nardina is living Vicky"

"Still at he hotel, I think Harry!"

"Were Robin and her having an affair?

"Harry, you know what Robin's like. He's a womanizer. I thought the two of us had something but he was only interested in what Victor was up to".

"Did Robin have something on Victor?

Vicky was not prepared for the question.

"Me and Vic have had difficult times and our relationship was going nowhere."

"I strayed Harry, Victor put all his time and energy into some business deal with Clive."

"What about Clive, Vicky. Do you think he's alive?"

Vicky was visibly shocked.

"I thought Clive was dead…but I saw him yesterday".

Harry felt relief. Could there be a breakthrough.

"Whereabouts, Vicky?

"Up in one of the nice bars, the Coral Reef, I think".

"Vicky, did you know what Clive and Victor were into?"

Vicky was hesitant.

"Harry, Victor kept a lot to himself, even his money!"

"He was always involved in things with the CRU - tobacco, booze and stuff; like that but I think he was to his arm pits in something really big."

"Drugs Vicky?"

"Maybe, don't know. Could be something else - weapons!"

Harry's ears pricked.

"Weapons, like terrorism?"

Vicky was out of her league.

"I don't know Harry, honestly".

Harry knew that Vicky had her limitations. She genuinely knew nothing more he thought.

"What you doing later Vicky?"

Vicky smiled.

"Is this a date Harry?"

"Stop teasing Vicky. We have some work to do and I thought we could have a meal out and see who we might come across. Interested?"

"Okay, Harry. Sorry about leading you on."

Harry looked at Vicky sympathetically.

"Vicky I want to find out where Victor is. I know you do. I want to help, okay."

"About 7.30 okay.

Harry had a problem. He had got some of his clothes back from the Rio Grande but he needed to have them washed. He also needed a shower.

Francesca had given him the run of her house and he knew she was out of town today.

The house was empty when he arrived. He fixed himself a drink from the cabinet. He thought he should eat and settled for some pasta. Harry put some clothes in the washer. He made his way out onto the patio and thought he might catch up on some sunshine.

Harry decided to give Warlord a ring.

~

The room was dark. No windows and there was a stale smell. Outside there was banging. A door squeaked and there was wind blowing hard. There were gushing waves.

Nardina was cold. She was blindfolded and her arms and legs were tied with rope. She felt dirty; she was inhaling her body odour.

Hunger was a pain that returned at more frequent intervals. She didn't know her captors.

Nardina didn't know how long she had been held in the room. Time was impossible to measure. Constant darkness.

She cried a lot and wondered why she had been held captive.

~

Warlord didn't answer his phone. Harry was a little surprised. His friend was more predictable than the weather.

Harry thought he would try him later.

Francesca had not returned from her business trip. He left the house at seven for the short journey to the Coral Reef.

Vicky looked stunning. She was drinking a Bloody Mary when he arrived. She smiled teasingly.

"Hi Harry, I'll get you a vodka". Harry liked to be in control and to have got his own drink. But he didn't mind.

Vicky was trying it on. Sex was on her agenda but despite her efforts Harry wasn't interested.

"Listen Vicky, let's get one thing straight. I am not going to bed with you tonight or any night. That's not on for me. Okay, sorry."

Harry couldn't have made it clearer as to how he felt about Vicky but she persisted throughout the evening. Harry ignored her.

His mind was thinking other things when he was interrupted.

The girl was tall, long black hair, eyes like sparkling jewels and a figure that attracted him to her. She was more than half his age. He remembered her from earlier in the day. She was one of the two receptionists from the Rio Grande, who caught his eye. He was now mesmerized by her.

He made for the bar to get drinks for Vicky and himself but he was more interested to get to know who this young beauty was. Harry had another motive. She might know about Nardina.

How could he get Vicky out of the way?

Vicky would suspect if he left now.

He wanted to meet this girl who was flashing her eyes at him. Harry was approaching 50 but he had no problem relating to women. He decided to live for the moment.

The girl was called Julie. She was English, but had Spanish parents. She had only started working at the Rio Grande. But she was bright and knew quite a lot about Sardinia.

Julie knew that Harry was a friend of Nardina and Clive and had no hesitation in talking to him. There was also chemistry between them. He needed to put things on hold.

He thought hard but decided to stick with Vicky and meet Julie for lunch tomorrow.

"I'll see you tomorrow, say 12.30 Julie, okay!" Harry gave her kiss on the cheek. Julie looked Harry straight in the eyes.

"See you Harry". Harry's heart was racing. He would have loved to spend some time with Julie but he needed to keep Vicky on board.

Vicky was put out by Harry's attention to Julie but didn't let on. She knew that Harry didn't fancy her but she was a woman with needs.

"Sorry about that, Vicky". Vicky didn't believe Harry.

"It's okay Harry, I know you like the new models!" They both laughed.

"Harry what plans have you got tonight?" Harry knew here he'd like to be.

"I would like to find out where Nardina is. Fancy going over to the Rio Grande Vicky?"

Vicky was staying at the Hotel and didn't mind. She hadn't given up on seducing Harry.

Most of the residents of the small hotel were out for the night. Benalmedina was alive with partygoers and couples out for a meal and a drink.

A young woman was on reception. She spoke fluent English but was unable to tell harry where Nardina was. Harry made his way to his hotel room. Vicky remained at reception to have a drink.

The neon signs outside lit up Harry's room. His bed had fresh linen and there was a perfume fragrance in the room. Out of the darkness of the bathroom a figure of a woman appeared.

"Harryee, where have you been. I've missed you around".

Francesca's dark complexion and black dress hid a mystery. Harry thought how beautiful she was but that somehow there was a sinister look about her.

"You weren't at the house when I got back. I thought we could go out for the rest of the night".

"I'm whacked Francie, really. I need my bed". Harry rubbed his eyes.

"Why go to bed on your own Harryee. There's room in there for me!"

Vicky lunged at him. Harry resisted; telling her that he needed to go down to reception. ....

"I'll go in the bathroom, see you soon darling". Harry would not resist her. He thought of Vicky and as much as he wanted to spend the night with Francesca he needed to find out where Nardina was.

When Harry got to reception Vicky had gone. He checked with the girl behind the counter but she hadn't seen Vicky leave.

Harry thought that Vicky had not been too pleased with Harry's pre-occupation with Julie earlier in the evening and had decided to leave.

Francesca's obsession was obvious. Harry was suspicious of her

"Harryee I have missed you". Francesca was rambling a lot. Harry was unsure as to whether she had been drinking, or had taken some drugs.

Francesca was talking in riddles. She was lying on top of the bed naked and was perspiring a lot.

"Harryee I have seen Clive tonight. He tried to…" Francesca's words were slurred.

"Tried to kill me, kill me". Harry was keen to find out more but his concern for Francesca increased.

"He held her close, attempting to prevent her falling unconscious.

"Francie, what happened tonight. Where was Clive?

Harry was giving Francesca water. He rang reception for some black coffee although he was unsure what she had taken.

"Harryee be careful. Clive and Victor are out to get you".

"Victor who?" Harry wanted to be clear whom Francesca was referring to.

"I just know him as Victor". Francesca lapsed into a coma.

Chapter 7
Sharks and Dinosaurs

Nardina's captors called on her every few hours and provided her with some basic nutrition. She hadn't washed for days and had a pride about her dress but it was being alone and isolated that frightened her most.

Senseless thugs but someone skilled at mind games did not manage her existence.

Nardina was being kept out of the way because she posed either a threat or an embarrassment.

There were two men holding her in a storage area of a disused shop unit close to Benalmedina. They were on the payroll but not the instigators. They were Spanish. Nardina was not frightened of them but they refused to answer her questions, or simply didn't have any answers.

❧

Harry kept Warlord in touch with developments and the news that Victor might be alive.

Warlord was wary of Harry's story. Even Harry thought it amazing, as his recollection of Victor's body lying in the shower was vivid.

Francesca had mentioned it. She had been drunk but why bring up Victor up? She had slept off whatever she had taken and was back in the fast lane.

Harry thought Francesca to be something of a mystery. She either had resilience or an acting ability. Harry was unsure of her motives or loyalties. He seemed sure she would be driven by financial reward.

❧

He had a thought. It had been some time since he had spoken to his long-term partner, Natalie Allan. Natalie was an outspoken but honest cockney. Harry could level with her and they had an open relationship.

Harry was addicted to women and Natalie accepted Harry's over-active libido. When they were together, the other women were incidental.

"Nat, fancy coming over here for a break". Nat had a hairdressing salon in Kentish Town.

"Yeah, could do with a break babe. I'm a bit sick of blow dry and the tittle tattle from all the old dames around here".

"What's wrong babe? Natalie was curious why Harry had rang her.

"I'm a bit confused about what's going on over here and I need you".

"Don't want to say too much on the phone."

"How soon can you come over Nat?"

"Can get a cheap flight and could be out by tomorrow night".

"Great". Harry was relieved and Natalie sensed it.

For the moment Harry had agreed to meet Julie at lunchtime. He had forgotten where they where to meet and he decided to go down to reception.

Julie's eyes followed his as he walked down the twisting staircase. The bright lemon low cut dress contrasted her long suntanned legs and brown eyes. She was sipping an iced bacardi.

"Where do you fancy going for lunch? Harry favoured a quiet rendezvous.

"I don't mind Harry, you choose. I have my car outside."

"Let's go for a drive then". Harry took her arm and they went to the waiting Audi dark blue convertible.

The road out of Benalmedina was dusty. They passed a number of shop units, some of which were boarded up and had lease signs displayed.

"You know anyway interesting Julie?" Harry put his hand on her knee. She didn't resist.

"I know somewhere about 2 kilos away that might be interesting. Quite high up overlooking the beach".

"Do you like sea food Harry?"

"Yeah, I do".

"Me too, it's a specialty at The Cove".

Harry's interest in the cuisine was secondary. He felt lust for Julie and she knew it.

The blue convertible made it's way up a dusty twisting track.

The Cove was a small beach hut, with basket seating. Done out in "Caribbean" style. Meals were served out from a barbecue.

It was a hot day but the temperature was simmering, due to the charcoal and wood.

There was only a handful of people at the bar.

Harry and Julie found a shaded spot nestled near to a palm tree. They had the opportunity for privacy.

"How do ya come to know this place Julie?"

"Ah my parents live about a kilo from here. You can see their house from here."

Julie pointed to a villa just down the hill from The Cove.

"They are away at present. Daddy has some business in Gibraltar and my mother never lets him out of her sight.

"Do you live with your parents Julie?

"No, not usually. I have an apartment in town but I am looking in on the place. I am an only child. No brothers or sisters to bother me".

"What about boyfriends?"

"You are a pretty girl Julie!"

Harry was holding her hand. Julie seemed embarrassed.

"Some men are just after what they can get. My parents are worth a bit and I have everything I want. But there are some things money can't buy."

Harry was keen to know why Julie was working at The Rio Grande. She didn't need the money!

"I like a bit of independence. My parents see me okay. I am studying business and languages at the university in Valencia. The Rio Grande provides the pocket money I guess".

"Do you know Nardina well".

Julie was a bit guarded.

"My mother has known Nardina a number of years. They're almost like sisters!"

" It was sad about Clive. I knew them both well".

"Yeah. I know, They were very close I think".

 Harry felt that Julie was hiding something. He pondered. Perhaps he was reading too much into what she said.

"I've been away at university the last two years and a number of years before I was working in England."

"Whereabouts Julie?

"I worked in Manchester and then up in Newcastle as a clerk with a firm of accountants".

Julie quipped.

"I like to travel but when I get my degree I think living in a warmer climate would suit me better".

"Yeah, you rarely get a sun tan in the North east of England!"

They both laughed, giving each other a hug and a kiss.

Julie was very attractive and Harry was giving her the eye. She was a little more guarded.

There was something different about Julie that Harry had not encountered with a lot of women. Normally, the women Harry knew responded to his charm. There was sophistication about Julie. She was a young woman, barely 30, with a lot going for her. Harry was at his peak.

Julie took Harry by surprise.

"Harry, do you know a man called Victor?"

Harry perked up.

"Victor who?"

"He's from a place near Newcastle. I s that far from where you come from Harry."

Harry didn't like questions, he wanted the answers."

"I know a number of Victors Julie. What's his surname?"

"Plum, something. Can't remember."

"He used to come over to the firm of accountants in Newcastle when I worked there. Seemed a nice guy!"

Harry was baffled by Julie's sudden interest in a man like Victor Plumtree.

"I saw him the other day here in Benalmedina."

"Is he a friend of yours Harry?"

For once Harry was lost for words.

Julie was clever and cool. Could she be trusted?

It was obvious to Harry that Julie was no easy prey. They drank and ate. Laughed a lot but the conversation threw up some food for thought.

Harry wanted to trust Julie but he wondered about Julie's connections. For once he wasn't sure about his next move.

An afternoon of passion was not on the cards but another meeting might be.

"Julie, I would like to spend more time with you but I have to go soon. Could we meet again soon."

"Sure. You're a nice guy. It would nice to have a drink one afternoon. Yeah, soon."

Harry's mind switched. Natalie's flight from Gatwick was due in at 6.30. A couple of hours to have a shower and get changed back at the Rio Grande. But he also had a phone call to make.

Warlord was having a few drinks with friends at the club. Harry could hear a live football match. Sport was always at the hub of activity.

"Harry, how ya doin' mate?"

"Listen Worrie, I need a proper talk about what's goin' on."

"Victor's alive and well."

"What Harry, I missed that. Victor what?

"Worrie, Victor is alive and over here".

"Bloody hell we need to talk Harry. Ring back in an hour can you?"

"Sure. "

~

Natalie's flight had been delayed. Harry waited around the busy entrance of Malaga airport. A sea of faces. Anxiety, frustration and a face in the crowd familiar to Harry. He was looking for Natalie but didn't expect to see Victor Plumtree.

Victor didn't want to see Harry but couldn't avoid eye contact. There was a strained smile but then suddenly he disappeared among the crowds.

Something to tell Warlord, Harry thought.

Just as Harry rang Warlord, there was a tug at the back of his neck.

"Hiya Harry." Natalie gave Harry a kiss and he felt the warmth of her face on his.

"Good to see ya Nat." Harry felt that for the first time he was with someone he trusted.

Natalie was in her early forties but her long blonde hair made her look youthful. Harry had known Natalie for about 10 years. There was a spark between them. He longed to run his fingers through her hair.

The Rio Grande was unusually busy. There had been a bullfight in nearby Fengirola. There was a part mood with sangria in plentiful supply.

Harry was relaxed in Natalie's company and his mind was at ease. He barely heard the sound of his mobile. It was Warlord.

"Harry what's this about Victor?" Harry held Natalie close.

"Victor's alive and well. I saw him tonight at the airport."

"Did he speak Harry?

"No, he disappeared before I could talk to him. But he's alive Worrie."

"Bloody hell Harry, what's goin' on?."

"I don't know Worrie but I'm goin' to find out."

"Worrie, find something out for me, will ya?"

"Yeah, what's that Harry?

"Find out about Victor's visits to some accountants in Newcastle and a woman called Julie."

"I thought there would be a woman in it somewhere Harry."

"Seriously Worrie, see what ya can find out."

"I know where Victor used to go. There's nothing I don't know."

"Find out about Julie, Worrie. I think she knows something about Victor and where he is."

"Okay Harry, leave it with me."

Harry told Natalie everything. He didn't seek advice but would have welcomed it. She knew better. Natalie liked Harry as the strong character he was. He was dominant in many ways.

"Harry, what are you goin to do."

"Nothing tonight, except lovin' you."

"Tomorrow's another day and Worrie might throw up some answers".

❧

Francesca returned. She had been away out of town on one of her many secret trips. The house was in darkness apart from a light in the lounge.

She was tired but wondered who the intruder might be. The front door was open. As she entered she saw the face of a young woman.

"Hello mother dear, how are you?"

"Julie it's you. Does your father know you are here?

"Where have you been the last few days. Been seeing Clive have you, or is they're someone else?"

"I've been seeing this guy. He's nice. The truth is I have fallen for him and I think he fancies me."

"Slept with him, have you?"

"Yes, if you must know."

"Has he got a name?"

"Yeah, they call him Harry."

Julie smiled. She enjoyed giving Francesca the third degree!

Francesca got angry with her.

"You know him don't you?"

"Yeah, he was with me this afternoon."

"And no, I didn't go to bed with him. I'm not like you."

"No, you're not are you Julie. You're just like your father. Cold and calculating."

"That's rich, coming from you mother. You're as cold as ice!

"Just get out Julie".

"I'll get out, but how much will you pay me to keep my mouth shut?"

"What do you mean Julie?"

"My dad doesn't know does he?"

"Doesn't know what Julie".

"That Clive's, my dad".

"He thinks it was…"

"Julie, your real dad was no one important. Just a fling with a boy in a night club."

"His name was Clive, wasn't it mother?

"No Julie it wasn't."

Francesca didn't sound believable.

"We'll see. Once I tell my dad."

"Don't Julie, please leave it. It's dangerous!"

"Be careful Julie and don't trust Harry, okay."

"Leave him to me."

Julie didn't trust the woman she knew as her mother. She had a mind of her own and planned to see Harry again.

⁓

Natalie and Harry had a long sleep. It was well into the early hours before sleep overtook sex.

"I see you've lost none of your old charm in the bedroom Harry."

Harry was smiling like the cat that got the cream.

"You're quite a woman Nat."

"When are you going back."

"Sick of me already. Got another woman lined up?"

"No. I would like you to stay for a while that's all".

"Harry, I've got to go back after the weekend."

"But I thought you might make at least a week of it".

Harry felt a little on edge and Natalie being around helped him.

"I'll see what I can do Harry. But no promises okay!"What's it worth"

"How about the rest of the morning in bed."

"Okay darling. You've only got a one track mind."

⌇

Warlord trusted Jerome Chance on some matters. Finding out about Julie's connections with Victor and anything else that might assist Harry.

"Worrie tell Harry to be careful. Julie's parents are into all kinds of deals, usually the murky type."

"What does that mean in simple terms Jerome."

"Francesca, Julie's mother had an affair with Clive about 30 years ago. She's his love child. Julie's out to get at her mother. Francesca is ruthless and very dangerous. She would kill if she had to protect herself. There is a lot for her to protect."

"What about Victor in all of this?"

"Victor and Clive have a scam going on in Gibraltar. I understand they have been involved in some illegal drugs and gun trade."

"Victor, Jerome you're joking aren't you?"

"No I 'm not Worrie. In fact our Police are looking for Victor. Some kind of business up in Newcastle, drugs related. That's all I know."

"Thanks Jerome. Keep me posted if you hear anything else".

"Will do. Promise me that you'll warn Harry. There are guns and drugs nd his life could be at risk."and his life could be at risk."

Chapter 8
Moving Targets

Harry decided to take Natalie out for a drive. He thought he would go up to The Cove. The venue did not hold any special feelings. The location was good and the food was enjoyable.

His encounter with Julie was not something he kept a secret from Natalie. Natalie understood that Julie could hold the key to a number of unanswered questions.

Harry and Natalie arrived at The Cove but the place was empty, apart from two barmen and a chef

"It looks like we've got the place to ourselves Nat."

"Red wine?"

"Yeah great thanks."

"They do nice seafood here".

"I'd prefer a nice steak, or maybe pasta Harry."

"I don't need an aphrodisiac darling!"

They both laughed loudly.

~

Francesca and Clive were at the airport. The short flight to Gibraltar was a regular trip for both of them. In fact Clive had contemplated a base on 'The Rock' but his business activities needed space and distance. The Spanish mainland was ideal. He was among a lot of like-minded people. Entrepreneurs like fish in an ocean. Some were legitimate.

Clive had been running the illicit organization for a number of years. He used various people to protect him. Francesca was also a perfect foil. She was involved in a number of legitimate operations and was ruthless, an important quality in business. Clive's military experience was a bonus. He had worked with explosives and following his Army career he maintained contacts.

Harry met Clive during a tour of Northern Ireland. They forged a friendship built upon survival. Clive had a fascination, even an obsession with weapons. His association with drugs was quite different. Clive had taken 'soft' drugs but saw a profit potential in trading cocaine and heroin.

Francesca was like Clive - hard hitting and brutal if she needed to. Most of all they were formidable, like 'Bonnie and Clyde'.

Clive's relationship with Victor Plumtree was less clear.

Victor's roots were firmly in his native Durham and the links with CRU. Victor saw Clive as a rich seam to exploit.

Robin's role in the organization cost him his life. He wanted to be the top guy but in reality he was a pawn and didn't like it.

∾

Warlord rang Harry and told him about His conversation with Jerome Chance.

"Harry be careful. Jerome reckons that your life could be in danger. Don't trust that hussy Julie."

Natalie was a great bonus for Harry but she had to return to London. Harry needed her to stay but she had to go back.

"Harry I'll come out again in a couple of weeks. Sorry I can't stay darling."

"Okay Nat but phone me okay".

Harry was determined to find Victor and confront him about his activities. He was convinced that Victor was deceiving Warlord and despised him for that.

He pondered: Nardina, where was she and did she play a part in the conspiracy?

"Nat, stay for a few more days. I need you."

Natalie had not heard Harry say this before. She was worried about him.

"Harry, I'll keep in touch."

Natalie was the only person Harry could trust and she was leaving him.

Harry had tried to persuade Natalie to stay. She·had suggested to Harry that he take a break and return with her to London.

Both of them decided that for the next few weeks they would sort out their business dealings and then head off for a break in Hong Kong.

Harry was confident that the seedy dealings involving Victor, Clive and whoever else could be exposed and then he would get out of Spain. The Far East was somewhere he'd never been to before but he fancied the oriental mood and culture.

He was sickening of Spain and had an appetite for new horizons.

~

Nardina's incarceration was getting her down. The routine of twice daily visits, having to eat when her captors dictated and being deprived of light and space, as well as the lack of the freedom was bearing down on her.

Other than her captors, no one had any interest in where Nardina was. She thought of her business and often her mind was filled with the memories she had of Harry.

Clive was a thorn in her side and she believed he had something to do with her kidnap. She was powerless trapped in her existence.

The warm temperatures of the summer and the increasing stench within the small room were unbearable.

~

Natalie left for London and Harry was a bit down. He would miss her but the most overwhelming emotion he had was frustration.

Harry needed to see Julie again but there were would be no sensitivity and little respect. He detected a hard streak in Julie that resembled a characteristic he saw in Francesca.

Growing tired of the Rio Grande, Harry decided on a drive. He thought that perhaps a change of scenery might help him think through strategy.

Harry traveled towards the highway that would take him to Valencia. He recalled Julie's association with the city, attending the university and although a bit of a long shot he wondered if he would turn up anything on Julie.

But there again, it was a long journey for a long shot. He wondered whether Julie might be at her parents' home and decided to go their first.

Harry had not been aware that Julie's mother was Francesca, but he knew there was a relationship between them. There were uncanny characteristics they shared.

The villa stood high looking outwards onto the Atlantic Ocean. Cypress trees concealed it. The property was large and there was a swimming pool at the front of the house. Various plants and flowers provided an array of colour.

There was a Shogun in the drive.

Harry rang the doorbell and a pretty young woman answered. She did not have a good command of English but told him there was no one at home.

"When is Julie back?"

"I'm not sure Signor. Can I tell her who called?"

"Yeah, say Harry called, okay!"

Harry wandered to his car and as he drove off he saw a small car drive towards him. It screeched to a halt.

"Hello Harry, what are you doing up here. Spying on me?"

"Why would I do that Julie. Have you something to hide?"

"How about coming back to the house Harry. I want to talk to you."

Harry struggled to restrain his interest.

Julie looked stunning in a bright orange dress. Her cleavage was more disposed than at their first meeting.

"Harry, this is Celestine, our housekeeper I guess. She's really part of the family.

Harry smiled.

Julie took him through to a sun lounge looking out the swimming pool. She peeled off her dress in front of him, which revealed a scanty bikini.

Harry didn't complain. Julie was teasing him and that was obvious to him.

"Got a drink Julie?"

She looked at him provocatively.

"Sure Harry, forgive me. Vodka and ice as I remember!"

Harry nodded.

"So you haven't forgotten me Julie."

"Not at all Harry. How could I".

Julie leaned over to give Harry a kiss.

Harry took his drink.

"Do you swim Harry?"

Julie pulled him towards her and they kissed passionately.

"I'm sure I will have some trunks or shorts belonging to daddy upstairs."

"Wait there!"

Harry took a look around the outside. There was a car at the back of the house that looked like the one Francesca was driving the last time he saw her.

"Harry. There are some shorts here. Do you need the bathroom?"

"Yeah sure!"

"Don't be long. I'm going in for a dip!"

When Harry came out Nardina was waving at him to come in to the pool.

Harry swam towards her. She had poured him a fresh drink and they sat by the pool. Harry fancied Julie and she knew that.

Teasing him back into the water they swam towards the other end of the pool. She untied the blue strap of the bikini and invited Harry towards her.

"Fancy making love to me underwater Harry?"

Harry didn't decline. She removed his shorts and they entangled intimately.

"You're some lover Harry. We must do this again!"

Julie and Harry got into some bathrobes, which Celeste had left beside two sun loungers

150

"Am I as a good as my mother Harry?"

Harry was gob-smacked. He tried to be complimentary.

"So your mum is Francesca I guess. You are very like her!"

"Is that a good thing Harry?"

"You're both very beautiful Julie."

"What a gentleman you are Harry. You're not bad for your age."

Julie giggled loudly.

"I like older men and as you know I like sex."

"So do I Julie!"

Harry was sitting next to Julie and they were holding hands.

"Who's your dad then?

Harry's directness caused Julie some amusement.

"I like your accent Harry. Quite sexy really."

"Well I have two dads really. Aren't I the lucky one!"

"You know Clive don't you Harry. He's my real dad. Him and my mother I mean".

"Robin was my other dad and he saw me through school and all that. He's dead now".

There was finality in Julie's voice but no emotion.

" Clive was a friend of mine. Him and Nardina seemed close."

"Have you been married Harry?"

"Yeah, didn't work out. But what about Clive and Nardina?"

"Just like you Harry they didn't work out. She hated the fact that they had no children and that I was a 'love child'.

"Nardina thought that Clive was killed on a fishing trip. The Police told her."

 "She was devastated Julie."

"Who was the man, if it wasn't Clive?"

"Just a nobody really. Daddy used to have quite a group with him and it was just one of the fishermen".

"The Police were pretty amateur really".

"Poor you Harry. You don't know the half of it."

"Nardina's no angel. I know you have a soft spot for her!"

"She always talks about you".

"Nardina killed Robin you know".

"I don't think so Julie."

Harry's response surprised Julie.

"Who do ya think killed Robin then?"

"I'm not sure but Nardina is not the killing sort".

Julie held Harry close.

"Everyone is capable of killing, Harry. You should know that!"

"You were in the Army and killing is part of the job."

"In active service Julie yes. That's different."

"What motive did Nardina have to kill Robin.

"She had more of a motive to kill Clive after what he did!"

"There's a lot you don't know Harry!"

Julie was not prepared for Harry's next question.

"You could have killed Robin, couldn't you Julie?"

"Don't be silly Harry. I'm offended by that!"

"I wouldn't kill anyone and not Robin. I loved him. He was my dad".

Tears flowed down her cheeks. Harry was not convinced by Julie's display. She was a drama queen. He doubted whether Julie loved anyone.

Harry looked at her with some intensity. Julie was unsure of herself.

"Sorry Julie I didn't mean to hurt you." Harry was inside her mind.

Julie kissed Harry again on the lips.

"Show me you care Harry. Take me to bed darling. You're so sweet."

Harry played with her. Caressing and groping her, he carried her upstairs for a sexual conquest.

Downstairs there were voices. It was a man and a woman.

"Clive are you there mate?"

Julie whispered to Harry.

"It's Victor and that bloody woman!"

"You're right what you say Julie. There is a lot I don't know!"

"I need to get out of here. It's sick!"

"Don't Harry. I need you here."

"Why Julie. You have it all. Nothing bothers you!"

"I'm off"

Harry made his way out on to the landing. Looking down the stairway he saw the man's face. It wasn't the face he expected.

Julie followed Harry to the top of the stairs.

"Hello Uncle Victor. What are you doing here!"

"Uncle Victor, eh. That's a new one Worrie!"

"What ya doin here!"

"Come to see what you're up to Harry. Just as I thought with a woman".

"I could do with a pint right now".

"Never mind the beer Worrie, or should I say Victor. What's goin' on?"

As Harry walked towards him a woman appeared.

"Well if it's not you Dilys. God, who the hell's running the club?"

"Harry's its not how it looks. We'll explain."

Harry had always got along well with Dilys and Warlord was his best friend.

Julie had gone off into the kitchen to make some drinks.

Harry and Warlord's eyes were locked. There was anger.

"Do you two know Julie?"

"Aye, she's a bonnie lass isn't she."

"Clever and all Harry."

"Shut up Worrie."

"How come ya know Julie."

"We met in Newcastle once with Victor."

"Really. Why did she call you Uncle Victor then?"

"Are you Vicky then Dilys."

"No Harry, it's nothing like that".

"Victor convinced us that his plan out here was good for the CRU and asked Worrie to be his 'double' or something. I had to be Vicky. Don't like that bit

Harry didn't respond to Dilys' attempts at humour.

"Harry, I have always been your mate but I knew, you wouldn't approve of Victor's plan."

"You're right about that Worrie."

"So where was Harry going to be in the plan?"

157

"Squeezed out I think".

Harry's anger increased.

"Never Harry. You would have got a slice!"

"How big a slice?"

"Victor's always done the finance!"

"Drugs and weapons you said Worrie!"

"I know I did but got it wrong Harry."

"You know nothin' Worrie."

"Victor's got you wrapped around his little finger."

Warlord had a vacant look.

"If you and Dilys are playing Bonnie and Clyde, Victor must be the Godfather."

"You've been duped Worrie."

Julie had disappeared out into the drive. She drove off in the blue Audi convertible.

"Harry let her go. She'll be meeting up with Clive. Victor's cut him out of the action."

"Julie doesn't know that though!"

"She knows something Worrie."

"What's that Harry."

"You're not Victor mate!"

Chapter 9
Racing Hearts

The plane from Gibraltar arrived at Malaga on schedule. Clive and Francesca looked quite casual mingling among holiday travelers.

No one would have suspected them. They walked together like uncompromising lovers. Carrying nothing but shoulder bags, their documentation was never checked by airport officials. Much of their energy and attention was on terrorist activity.

Julie's appearance at the airport was unusual and caused Clive and Francesa some concern.

"Hello mother. Have a good trip."

Clive had a discerning look.

"What are ya doing here babe?"

"Uncle Victor came to the house this afternoon with that woman."

"So what's wrong with that Julie?"

"Uncle Victor often comes over."

"Unusually daddy because Uncle Victor was someone else."

"Someone called Worrie and the woman wasn't Vicky but someone called Dilys."

"Harry knew them."

"Harry was there Julie, why?"

Francesca was quite agitated.

"Julie. What was Harry Farmer doing at the house?"

"He came to see me."

Both Clive and Francesca's anger erupted.

"I don't like the sound of this."

"The last person I want involved is Harry."

"You know him then Clive?"

Francesca was pensive.

"Yeah, very well. We were in the Army together and came to visit Nardi and me at the Rio Grande."

"I hope you haven't given anything away Julie?"

"You must know Harry likes women and likes to exploit them".

"Daddy, you make him sound like a monster!"

"Harry's a charmer but he's no fool Julie."

Julie looked at her mother's face. There was no doubting her unease. She didn't know about Clive and Harry but she feared her relationship with Harry would get out.

～

Harry felt a bit sorry for Warlord. He saw his vulnerability. But he was also annoyed that he hadn't trusted him He wondered about Julie as well and what she might do and say to Clive and Francesca.

"Harry, I am not sure what to say. Sorry mate."

"I feel let down Worrie. I thought we were friends."

"Trouble is Worrie. You might have sounded the alarm for Clive and we could get squeezed."

"I'd agreed to meet Victor in the morning in some bar called the Coral Reef. Do ya know it Harry?"

"Yeah, I do Worrie. You go but I'll stay close by, okay?"

"It's important I keep out of sight, but if you need me Worrie give me a shout right!"

"I don't know how to handle Victor. He's bloody 'double-crossed' us Harry."

"Stay cool Worrie, or he'll be suspicious. Just listen to what he has to say."

" Give me a ring Worrie and we'll meet. Right?"

"Okay Harry!"

"Don't be taken in Worrie by Victor and look after yourself."

"Cheers Harry."

Dilys had been unusually quiet but felt she had to intervene.

"Don't worry Harry, I'll keep the bugger right!

"Right, see you both later!"

Worrie and Dilys stayed at the Rio Grande. Harry seemed to have the run of the place in Nardina's absence.

~

Harry thought that Warlord looked totally out of place in Benalmedina. He didn't blend too well with the climate or surroundings. His dark blue shorts and tee shirt revealed a sun starved body. A Reebok sports cap covered his head. Dilys was less conspicuous wearing a light blue vest and shorts. She had obviously made use of a sun bed in Coxburn before making the trip.

Warlord was easy prey for Victor. Outside his normal domain he had already fallen foul of Victor's manipulation.

Harry tracked Warlord and Dilys but was conspicuous. Sporting a Nike cap, Harry followed Warlord who was walking quite heavily on his right side. The Coral Reef, which was only short distance from the Rio Grande.

There weren't many people around the bar restaurant, which came alive at night. He thought that Victor must have sneaked into the building, or was heavily disguised. Warlord had arranged to meet

Victor at 11. Harry decided he would gatecrash after about 10 minutes.

Close to the Coral Reef there was a small British bar. Harry had a bottled Kronenberg and kept watch.

He heard a faint voice coming from a nearby building. There were a couple of vacant shop units close to the small bar. It was the sound of a woman crying. Harry sensed that it was the unit next door. There was a voice, which he recognized.

The barman serving Harry a second bottle of Kronenberg looked suspicious. A young man with a distinct cockney accent tried to divert Harry's attention. Harry was in control. No one was going to distract him.

Harry put the young man on the spot.

"Did you hear a voice mate?"

"Voice, what voice!" His voice was shaky.

Harry was not convinced.

"Look mate. Have you got a hearing problem?"

Harry leaned over and caught the young man by the arm.

"You know something, don't ya?"

The young man tried to back away, holding up his hands in protest.

Suddenly, a heavy bald headed man appeared from behind the bar, dressed in a chef's outfit. There were no words but a frenzied fracas erupted.

The young man presented no threat to Harry, falling to the ground after Harry's body punch. The heavyweight was no pushover.

Harry had little time for fighting but he was keen to find out if the woman inside the locked unit was Nardina. He decided he would flee the bar and come back with reinforcements.

Seeing if Warlord was safe was a priority. But the bouncing chef was keen to prolong the brawl.

The fight moved out into the street. Harry winded the heavyweight and followed up with a right hook.

Harry heard Warlord's voice. Dilys rushed forward and clocked the big man as he struggled to his feet.

"Are you alright Harry?"

"Yeah Worrie!"

"Where's Victor?"

"The bugger didn't turn up Harry. Been warned off I guess!"

"Could be right!"

"Anyway, pleased ya turned up. Nardina's locked up in that place over there".

"Clive's missus?"

"Yeah Worrie. If we find her we might find Victor."

"Let's go then!"

Harry dragged his wounded attacker over to the bar, kicking him hard when he resisted.

"I need some answers. Who's that woman in there?"

"Don't know what ya talking about mate. No woman in there!"

"I am not stupid. You two dimwits know something."

The younger man was standing in front of the bar. Harry waved him aside.

"Look you can do this my way or spend some time in hospital!"

The two men were father and son and had access to the vacant property.

"We were hired by this woman to look after this woman. Keep her locked up but feed her every few hours".

"How long she been in there?"

"A couple of weeks."

"She's okay!"

"I'll be the judge of that. Has she been fed yet?"

"Yeah, we were goin' in with some lunch."

"Right, let's go in!"

Harry had the situation in hand but Warlord was around just in case.

Victor and Clive were playing golf and considering their next move. They were not unduly worried. They held all of the cards in the pack!

"All the fools are together now. Nardina knows nothing and Worrie's shown his card. He's with Harry".

Victor had decided that with Clive and himself running things, the CRU could be squeezed out. Few people knew they were still alive and they would have no one chasing them. Francesca was sound and loyal and Julie would not rock the boat.

Vicky could not trace him and he had no desire to see her again.

"What about Vicky. Will she be a problem Victor?

Clive was keen to have a life with Francesca and his daughter. Nardina was out of the way and in the frame for Robin's murder.

"Vicky's a pushover Clive."

Victor rarely smiled. Humour was not a prominent characteristic.

"I would have liked to see her face when she looked into the coffin and I was not in there."

"The greedy cow is going to get nothing and that will make her mad."

" I thought she was already mad Victor!"

The two men laughed and didn't have a care. The sun was scorching. Victor's thoughts were miles away.

"What's wrong Victor?"

"Ah nothing Clive. Just thinking about the rain and wind back in Durham. If they could all see me now that sad lot."

∼

Nardina was screaming hysterically when she heard Harry's voice.

"Harryee, Harryee let me see you. I missed you.

Nardina hugged Harry and wouldn't let him out of her sight.

"Who are they Harryee?"

"Ah Nardi this is my best mate Worrie and Dilys. They cam over to see Victor. You know Victor don't ya?"

Warlord and Dilys nodded.

"Don't mention that name Harryee. He's a dangerous man. I need to tell you…."

"Save it for now Nardi!"

"As long as you're okay. Let's get of here."

Harry and Warlord collared the two men and threatened them if they said anything. Privately, they knew that Clive and Victor would know that they were on their case.

To Warlord what he had experienced was like something out of a movie scene. It was more than the usual slice of action that running the CRU served up.

"Let's go and have something to eat." Warlord was lost for words momentarily.

Nardina was shaken and held on to Harry like a magnet. They followed close behind Warlord and Dilys.

"Tell you what Worrie, we'll go to this place I know."

"Can you get a nice sirloin steak and chips in there?"

"Sure Worrie, sure!". Harry looked up to a cloudless sky. A smile emerged.

There was a lot to talk about. Harry needed to have some answers from Nardina. Then there was Victor and Clive, elusive and hell-bent on squeezing out Warlord and Harry.

Nardina was distressed. Affected by weeks of captivity, she was not keen on being seen publicly. She was grateful to Harry and his friends and wanted to repay them.

"Why don't you come to the Rio Grande and we'll eat there. Is that okay?"

Food was the last thing on Harry's mind.

"That's fine!"

Seeing Nardina again filled Harry with mixed emotions. He was fond of her but she was a killer. It was definitely her face he saw in Robin's house. She must have killed him. He thought hard.

Nardina arranged food at the hotel. She was home again. A shower and some fresh clothes refreshed her. She looked stunning; Harry's heart was racing. He tried to disguise his feelings.

The meal satisfied everyone. Warlord got his steak and chips!

There was a lot to talk about.

"Nardi, what's been happening with you and Clive?"

"I know Clive's alive so don't make me out to be a fool."

Nardi looked shocked and confused.

"I don't know what ya mean Harryee." Nardina's response seemed genuine.

Warlord and Dilys were captivated. They were passive onlookers.

"So how did you end up in that place?"

"I don't know Harryee. I was out walking and two men I think grabbed me."

"I didn't see their faces. They came from behind me and the rest, I don't know."

To Harry's surprise Warlord joined the interrogation.

"When did you last see Clive?"

"But Clive he is dead. You know that Harry."

"I thought I knew that Nardi but I know he is alive."

It was obvious to Harry that Nardina didn't know about Clive.

"Who told you Harryee that Clive was alive?"

"Francesca. You know her don't you?"

"Should do Haryee. She's been blackmailing me!"

"Blackmail. How and why?"

"Clive had a love child to Francesca. When Clive died she wanted some money".

"But why come to you Nardi. Why not Clive?"

175

"The business was mine for tax. Every thing still is mine."

"So Clive wants back what he thinks is his?"

Nardina was stronger and determined.

"I will never let him have what I worked hard for Harryee."

"You're the only one I want to share anything with."

Harry was surprised but flattered.

Warlord and Dilys sat in amazement.

"Listen Nardi, I like you but…"

"Why did you kill Robin?"

"Robin is dead?

"When Harryee, how."

"Nardi, you were there and you killed him."

"I didn't Harryee. I kill no one. I couldn't kill anyone."

"But Robin he is dead. Poor man."

"So you knew him Nardi?"

"Yes knew him but kill him, no."

"Harryee, you have to believe me. Please!"

"Tell me something Nardi."

Harry looked into Nardina'e eyes.

"Who is Francesca really?"

"The truth Nardi please!"

Nardina started to shake and cried out.

"Francesca is my twin sister. I hate saying that word."

"Sister!"

"She always hated me. Wanted what I had. Clive, and money."

"When we were young she seemed jealous of what I had.

" She was a rebel and I was closer to my parents."

"Francesca hated that."

177

"I think she would do anything."

"Yes, maybe she and Clive had me locked up in that place".

"Nardina, you have to help us."

"Warlord and me need to get to Clive and Victor. They are out to get us as well."

"I'll see Harryee."

"But we have to work together Nardi. No going off anywhere."

"There have been enough disappearing acts Nardi."

Warlord blurted out a question.

"Do ya know Vicky?"

"Vicky, yes she liked Robin. Fancied him I think. She is no one."

"Know where she is Nardi."

Harry was impressed with Warlord.

"She was staying here a few weeks ago but I don't know since then."

"Can ya find out Nardi?"

Chapter 10
Closing In

The morning sun cast an amber glow over the bedroom. It was warm outside and the prospects for a hot balmy day beckoned.

Harry had succumbed to Nardina's charms and they had spent a passionate night together at the Rio Grande. As much as he wanted to lie beside her, there was business to be done.

"Nardi, I'm goin' out and I'll be back in a couple of hours."

"Don't go Harry. I need you."

"Nardi, Clive and Victor are taking us for a ride. I have some people to see!"

Nardini knew that when Harry had his mind set on something he would not give up.

"Take care Harry." Nardina gave Harry a kiss.

"Don't be long. I'll have some champagne on ice waiting for you."

Nardina's was provocative, gazing hard at Harry. He wanted to make love to her. She wanted him so much the radiance of her eyes were laser like.

Holding her close, she sensed danger and clung to him for fear she would not see him again.

"Watch yourself Harryee. Clive has weapons, guns. Just be careful darling."

Tears ran down her cheeks.

Harry joked with her.

"Listen Nardi. No one messes with Harry Farmer. No one!"

Deep down Harry sensed danger too. But he was determined as well. He rose to the challenge when the chips were down.

Warlord and Dilys slept in separate rooms. They were like brother ands sister.

Harry called in on his friend.

Dilys was sleeping in an adjoining room.

"Bloody hell Harry, what time is it?"

"About 10 o'clock Worrie. I want you and me to pay some people a call."

Warlord perked up, rubbed his eyes and headed for the bathroom.

"I'll put some coffee on shall I Worrie?"

"Aye, do that Harry. The tea isn't up to much!"

Warlord fancied tucking into breakfast. Harry wanted an early charge on Clive and Victor.

"We'll grab a sandwich Worrie and I'll buy you a steak later, okay mate?"

"I'm not much good on an empty stomach Harry but I'm up for free dinner!"

"But where are we goin' to go?"

Harry turned to his friend.

"You might know Worrie!"

"What do ya mean Harry?

"C'mon Worrie. I'm not stupid."

Warlord looked confused.

The two men stopped off for a burger. They didn't sit down at the café but kept walking.

"When you and Dilys came over here you went somewhere didn't ya?"

"I couldn't see you and Dilys just turn up. You've never been to Spain before have ya?"

"Alright Harry."

"Vicky rang me. She said you'd met her but then you got off with some woman…."

"And Worrie. Thought we were mates."

"We are Harry. Good mates!"

"So why didn't ya tell me about Vicky?"

"Well, I was goin' to but then there was so much happening and then all that stuff with Nardina and that."

"Sorry mate."

"No more secrets Worrie right!"

Warlord was looking down and didn't reply.

"Worrie, I mean that."

"Okay Harry."

"So where is she?"

"I know she's left the Rio Grande Harry and I think she's with Victor."

"Really, how sure?"

"Vicky is useless without Victor and also she has a score to settle."

"What do ya mean Worrie."

"Victor tricked her Harry. She hadn't banked on a coffin full of booze and tobacco!"

"Well, that's possible Worrie but what if Vicky was part of the ploy mate?"

"Putting on the act for the CRU and the Coxburn folk".

Warlord had a mystified look.

"You really think that Harry?"

"It's a possibility that's all."

"Worrie you have to look at all options."

"There's something I don't understand Worrie."

"What's that Harry?"

"Why did Vicky ring you?

"I don't know mate."

Harry believed that Warlord was gullible but he knew that he knew something about Vicky and Victor's whereabouts.

"If Vicky is lost without Victor how has she survived over here?"

"Robin was helping her out before he got bumped off."

"Yeah and…"

"What ya getting at Harry. You'd think you didn't trust me!"

"Worrie, Vicky knows where Victor is, right!"

"Or she's been with him all the time."

"Then of course there's Francesca and Clive."

"What do ya mean Harry?"

"You've got me confused."

"I'm confused Worrie because Julie thought you and Dilys were Victor and Vicky."

"I wonder why that was?"

"But I'm not Victor am I Harry."

"You know that and so do I but Julie thought you were."

"Why was that Worrie?"

Warlord's face was drained.

"I went with Victor once to this office in Newcastle. A firm of accountants Victor used to go to and that Julie worked there."

"Yeah, but she called you Victor!"

"That's cos Victor said he was somebody else."

"Who did he call himself Worrie/"

Harry was getting impatient.

"He told her he was somebody called Kevin, Kevin Robson."

"Poor bloody Kevin. Serves a good pint and has the patience of a saint."

"Bloody Victor, he uses people like condoms."

"Except he doesn't know how to use condoms Harry."

Harry restrained his laugh.

"Worrie, this is getting us nowhere."

"What are we goin' to do now Harry?

"Go for a drive and see if we can find Julie."

~

Nardina was sleeping when there was a knock at the door. She moaned and thought of Harry, thinking he was at the door. Her heart raced. Rushing to the door she was surprised to see the image before her.

"Clive what are you doing here?"

Clive had a gun. He was angry and the gun was concentrating his mind.

"Nardi, you have not seen me here. I want you to promise me..."

"I'll pay you £200,000 to keep out of my life Nardina. Never want to see you again.

"But Clive is a life worth so little?"

"What's it got to do with money Clive?"

"Plenty Nardina. You have a lot already and I have nothing."

"So how can you afford £200,000 Clive?"

"Why not pay me half a million?"

"You can afford it Clive."

"I can't Nardi, you have to believe me!"

"Why should I believe you?"

"I want half a million for what you've put me through Clive. Nothing less!"

There were two gunshots that ricochet off the walls of the bedroom. Clive and Nardina fell to the floor. A dark shadow hung over the couple who once enjoyed life together.

~

Harry and Warlord drove up to the house where Julie took him. Harry looked ahead and there was Julie's Audi was in the drive. His mind wandered for a moment.

Warlord noticed Harry's pre-occupation.

"What's wrong Harry?"

"I am just thinking that it's odd Worrie that this house belongs to Francesca and Clive and I don't know."

"Know what mate."

" I have been to another house where Francesca lives or is supposed to live."

"So, they have two houses. Some kind of tax dodge?"

"Possibly Worrie but could be that it's a cover, like where Victor is hanging out."

"Right, got ya Harry."

Warlord trusted Harry. He knew he could sniff out trouble. Warlord knew he was out of his depths. He was far removed from the familiar territory in Durham.

The two men sat in the hired Mitsibuishi and pondered their next move.

"Listen Harry, this is your call. As long as we get to that bugger Victor."

"No one is gonna rip us off Harry, no one!"

"I'm no loser Worrie, you should no that!"

The car wheels spun and as Harry accelerated he felt a burst of adrelenin..It was like those hairy moments weaving between the terrorist and the martyr. He thought of bravery and Rick McFadden. Rick was an Irishman who feared little and as a Sargeant Major there were those who shrieked at the sound of his voice as it bellowed across the parade ground.

Walking through fire was not Harry's style but he respected acts of bravery. He had seen fit men in combat reduced to carnage. Demented by the desperate acts of treachery, there were those who were the enemy who hovered like vultures across the lines but it was those who perched like allies whom the venom of a viper.

The enemy confronted and the strike was predictable. It was the unknown enemy who failed to comply with conventional battle.

Victor had become like Clive venomous. He'd always been cowardly and deceiving. Hell bent on a cunning plan and seeking the treasure.

Harry hated those who were disloyal. The CRU was as important to him as his business in Spain. He trusted Victor and Clive. But for them to destroy the CRU was to crush his best mate Warlord. He wouldn't tolerate that. Victor and Clive had to be eliminated. Their existence was a poisonous vein.

Looking across at Warlord sweating profusely. The dehydration being a condition he associated with heavy drinking, not excessive heat.

Harry was conditioned to the Mediterranean heat. He adored the sun beating down on his skin. The good feeling it radiated and the images of beautiful women clad in skimpy bikinis with golden suntans. He thought of the women in his life. That he loved others he was unsure about and those who deceived him.

The Mitsubishi pulled up outside the villa. The blue Audi was stood in the driveway. Another vehicle, a VW Passat was lined up alongside it.

Warlord had been asleep but as the vehicle came into view he jumped up and choked on his breath,

"Bloody Hell Harry. It's Victor's car."

"The black car Worrie?"

"Yeah, that's right. Always said when he had some real money he would get a Passat".

"We'll go in Worrie, but slowly."

"You wait here and I'll have a look around."

"Okay harry. Be careful mate and don't be long."

"You're not frightened Worrier are you?"

"No, but I don't know anyone and cannot trust…"

Harry's mobile rang out. Warlord looked at the illuminated signal.

It read: 'VP'.

Warlord opened the car door but had lost sight of Harry.

He saw the top of Harry's weaving like a commando among the cypress trees A single gun shot rang out.

Warlord pushed his head low under the glove compartment. He felt vulnerable, ambushed and fearing Harry was in danger, he clambered across the wide seat. Clutching the steering wheel Warlord attempted to engage the gears. Turning the key he revved up and drove off down towards the villa.

As he sped off Harry's face emerged. Crouched and nursing his leg, he limped towards the moving vehicle. Warlord plunged his weight on the brakes.

"Just drive Worrie, drive!"

Harry climbed into the passenger seat. His leg was grazed with some blood seeping through his light blue denims.

"I'm okay Worrie but that bitch Francesca is a demon!"

As the Jeep advanced down onto the track leading to the highway the sight of Francesca in the Audi convertible came into view. She had a crazed look about her.

"Follow her Worrie. Put yer foot down mate!"

The Jeep was in eager pursuit as Francesca drove towards Benalmedina.

~

The Rio Grande was unusually busy. There was laughter and the din of a crowd enjoying the end of a summer break. It was a traditional Spanish evening at the hotel. Jugs of sangria and portions of paella cooked in large pans filled the main reception area. The aura was mouth watering.

Upstairs on the second floor, two bodies lay huddled together on the couch. The room was in darkness, only the flickering lights from the street gave a hint of life.

The feint sounds of voices downstairs lingered. There was heavy breathing. A small patch of blood on the cream mosaic rug lay beneath the bodies of Nardina and Clive.

Clive was dead. A single shot to his chest shattered an artery. Nardina's right arm had a flesh wound but the agonizing pain was from the bullet lodged between her shoulder and lower neck.

Nardina longed for Harry to return. She needed him more than ever.

In the dining room downstairs amidst the carnival atmosphere a fracas enveloped. It was not expected. Some bars and hotels attracted a 'yob' culture but the Rio Grande was different. Couples and families wined and dined. The restaurant prided itself on catering for a variety of culinary tastes.

The site of the two bald men was not only a distraction but distasteful. Their bright blue vests were stained with stale perspiration. They bounded in and were shouting.

"Where's Harry and his bit stuff. She runs this gaffe?"

Sanchez walked over to them and tried to calm them down. They threw him aside before he could reason with them.

Rampaging through the hotel, they displayed the instincts of wild boar. There seemed little purpose in their outrage. Nardina was upstairs with serious injuries. Clive's decomposing body lying beside her.

Harry and Warlord had followed Francesca at high speed. The spectacle aroused great interest from the passing crowds. Even the local Policia cast an eye.

Francesca's car screeched to a halt. Slamming the door, she stormed into the busy hotel.

Harry and Warlord decided to follow her in but kept watch from the foyer of the Rio Grande.

"What's she up to Harry?"

Francesca saw the two blundering bald men but for a passing glance she ignored them.

She knew that Clive had come over to have it out with Nardina. She was very jealous of her younger sister and thought he might be wooed by her innocent charms.

Francesca had driven Clive to the edge. She had demanded that he get rid of her for good. Nardina was not a loving sister but a bitter rival.

A financial pay-off was not something she wanted.

"Where's Nardina?"

Sanchez was dazed after his encounter with Bummer and Grinder. Their ploy had worked. Disruption making way for Francesca's frenzy.

"Come on Sanchez, where?"

"Dun know Signorita!"

Bummer and Grinder had their orders. Jack Flashman was calling the shots or at least organized the fracas. But he was incapable of being the mastermind.

The two heavyweights came over towards Francesca and Sanchez.

"Do ya want him turned over?"

Francesca didn't want their help. They had done their job and were now an embarrassment.

"Just go. I can handle things my way."

Francesca made her way upstairs to Nardina's apartment.

Harry stormed in ahead of her.

"What ya doing Francesca."

His voice bellowed. Warlord stood close to him.

Francesca ran ahead of him.

Harry's mobile phoned rang.

"Take that Worrie will ya."

"Whatever Harry. It's Victor!"

"You talk to him."

Harry was in pursuit of Francesca.

"What's up Victor. Where are ya?

"Having a pint in Coxburn Worrie1"

"You're dead. You and that Romeo, Harry Farmer."

"You backed a loser Worrie."

Warlord went cold.

Chapter 11
Searching for the loot

Victor's return to Coxburn had been unexpected to most of the punters, apart from Jack Flashman and Trevor Pike. They felt they had masterminded Victor's return. They were a gullible pair. Victor was capable of mapping his own destiny.

Not everyone in Coxburn saw Victor as a son returning home. Warlord and Harry were popular.

Bob Snow was restrained and this was unusual for him. The Blackstone boys watched in trepidation as Victor assumed power.

Trevor Blackstone pondered.

"Wonder if Harry and Worrie are okay."

"They'll be back, you can be sure about that kid."

"Don't count on that you lot. I'm in charge now."

"Worrie and Harry. They're history and dead."

Bob Snow looked up over his pint. The smoke from his cigar was clearing but a ring hovered in the air for a while.

"They'll be back. You cannot kill them two buggers off that easy."

"Bob, you live in fantasy island mate. They're dead."

"Jack and Trevor's lads will have seen them off!"

"What them two morons. They only thing they should see off is their body smell."

"Watch it Bob!"

Trevor knew his son had little about him but brawn but he was his flesh and blood.

"Bob you're gettin' on a bit so I'll not not land ya one!"

"Not that old Trevor. I could teach ya a few moves!"

"Yeah, okay Bob. We'll just leave it eh!"

The smile on Bob's face hinted victory.

Gary and Trevor decided to milk it a little more.

"I'd say Bummer and Grinder would make two good mechanics, eh kid!"

"Yeah maybe. Wouldn't get my car serviced though."

"Why not Gary."

The two brothers were on a roll.

"If you needed a new exhaust it might some how come out of the engine. Wrong side up."

There were roars of laughter.

"Alright you've had you're laughs. Just remember I know who you all are!"

Flashman was deadly serious.

"C'mon lads cool it!"

Kevin Robson had a firm but calming voice. He prided himself on keeping good beer and sorting out any trouble.

~

Francesca burst through the door leading to Nardina's apartment. She wasn't prepared for what she saw.

"You scheming cow."

"Clive, Clive!"

"What have you done Nardi. Clive's dead."

Francesca went into hysterics. She started punching her sister but Nardina had fallen unconscious.

Harry entered the room.

"I think you need to explain yourself Francesca."

"Wouldn't you like to know lover!"

Francesca's voice lacked warmth.

"You're no lover to me. Just a bit of fun!"

Harry was angry. He was not in the habit of losing it with women but he realised how evil Francesca was.

"You killed Robin Francesca and Clive and who else. Money rules you!"

"And you're so innocent darling."

There was something evil about Francesca. She was more than just a selfish woman. Harry wanted to know so much.

"So where's Victor Francesca."

"Not in Spain Harry."

Warlord was out of breath. Running was not normality for him.

"He's in Coxburn Harry. Just rang me. Thinks his won!"

"Lopez, what you doin' here?

"Francesca I am arresting you for murder!"

"I like a man in a uniform!"

"A funny man as well."

"This is no joke signorita. You're under arrest.

Juan Lopez was the investigating officer in a murder case. He had also been at one time Francesca's lover.

Harry needed to clean up and make sure Nardina was all right. He went in the waiting ambulance to hospital but he had little time to waste.

Nardina would need a blood transfusion and emergency surgery to remove the bullet but she would survive.

Before she went to theatre Nardi asked Harry to kiss her.

"Harryee come back soon to me. I need you."

"Okay, Nardi. Take care and get well. See ya soon!"

"You'll not see her again Harry will ya?"

Warlord knew Harry. Not a one woman man.

"You like her though don't ya Harry."

"Yeah, I do, very much Worrie."

"I might come back."

But Harry and Warlord had an immediate destination in mind. Getting the quickest flight out of the Costa del Sol.

Waiting in the airport departure lounge Harry and Warlord had a drink together.

"Harry we have been mates a long time. The last few weeks have seen us in a few scrapes."

"Ya could say that Worrie and it's not over yet!"

~

With Francesca locked up in prison and Clive dead, Julie was in a precarious position. But to Victor she was an asset.

As well as having access to Clive's business accounts, she was intelligent and attractive. Very important qualities to a man who was lacked any. Even his choice of women was suspect. Vicky would hardly won anything in the beauty stakes and little did he know that as well as her infidelity, Vicky was an informer. She couldn't help herself. Discretion was not something she understood.

If Victor thought he could control Julie he was mistaken. She would play him along. After all, she was Francesca's daughter.

Julie missed the warm climate. Northeast winds were not something she was used to. Coxburn was hardly steeped in palm trees and olives!"

It was not the village Julie had come to visit. She had made many friends in Newcastle when she worked for a firm of accountants but her networks were not confined to work. She was a keen party animal and connected to many big money people.

There was a lot Julie knew about the area and what she didn't know she researched. She had big ideas but to her they were realistic. No one should underestimate her cunning and she had the capacity to have the CRU in the palm of her hand without knowing it. It would take a clever operator to combat her plans.

∽

Harry and Warlord arrived at Newcastle Airport without delay. They didn't expect any fuss as they passed through customs and out into the spacious arrival suite.

"Hello Harry, remember me."

The voice was familiar. It was young and fresh. Vivacious thought Harry.

"Julie, what are you doing here?"

"Same as you Harry!"

"What do ya mean Julie?"

"I know Clive, my dad is dead and that my mother is being held in prison for his murder."

"My mother didn't kill my dad Harry."

"Okay Julie, who did then?"

"I think you did, or maybe Worrie over there!"

Julie was pointing at the two men and to an outsider she sounded plausible.

"I can understand you being upset Julie. You loved your dad but you have to be believe me I didn't kill him."

"I'm not the murdering type Julie."

"But you had the motive to kill him Harry!"

"Did I Julie. What motive?"

"He was out to put pressure on Nardina and you and her have athing going don't you?"

Harry looked Julie straight in the eye. He saw a lot of Francesca in her but he recalled his first meeting with Julie and he had been cool and calculating then.

"So you're off to Coxburn are you?"

Harry was suspicious. He knew Julie knew Coxburn through her association with Victor but there was something sinister about her.

"Fancy meeting up later Harry?"

Warlord looked at Harry with a feigned look.

"Yeah harry maybe Julie fancies coming over to the club later."

"Thanks Worrie. I would love to."

Harry was unsure about Warlord's intentions.

"Okay Julie, see ya later okay!"

Julie went outside to a waiting car. There were two women in the back of the silver Merecedes. Darkened glass revealed their identity.

~

"Worrie, what the hell are ya playing at?"

"Nothing Harry. Just being hospitable."

There was a cheeky grin on Warlord's face.

Coxburn was lively most evenings but it was Friday and the weekend. The club would be packed out and the limited choice of fast food takeaways would be busy.

Harry and Warlord were hungry. The in-flight meals weren't substantial. They settled for an Indian Chicken Vindaloo in a nearby restaurant. Two cold beers cooled the hot spices.

There was nothing to cool their temperament as they anticipated a meeting with Victor. But who else would be at the welcoming reception.

Harry did not want a dramatic entry, so as not to alert Victor and his cohorts. The club had four main rooms. A small bar at the entrance, leading to a poolroom and bar and a spacious lounge at the rear. Upstairs there was a functions room. There was a singer and group belting out a sixties medley.

Harry and Warlord settled for the small bar and weighed up the scene.

"A pint of John Smiths mate and a Kronenbourg for Harry."

Kevin, the club steward was delighted to see the pair.

"Nice to see ya lads. This place has not been the same."

"Keep ya voice down Kevin."

"Okay, I understand!"

Kevin gazed through to the large lounge where Victor, Flashman and Pike were becoming increasingly inebriated.

"Good pint Kevin. The Spanish cannot keep smooth beer!"

Harry remained quiet. ; Just a glancing smile.

"Worrie I think we need to show some muscle."

"But I've just had a pint. I need a few more before I can get going Harry."

"Be serious Worrie. Them lot through there thinks we're dead. Let's show them mate."

"Aye, all right Harry."

~

They were a strange combination. Vicky, Dilys and Julie were drinking schnapps in a fancy bar on the quayside. The area had been renovated in recent years transforming it from a once thriving maritime site to a trendy up market development. They were hundreds of miles from Benalmedina, but the women had formed an alliance, each having their own motives for success.

Vicky would do anything to gain revenge on Victor. The humiliation of a funeral and a coffin without his body in and playing on her feelings hurt.

Dilys had been friends with Vicky since they went to school and considered the prospects of the high life a greater temptation than the drudge of Coxburn Club. No more punters bad-mouthing would be bliss in itself!

Julie was the mastermind. She was driven by success; life in the fast lane was risky but provided the life she yearned for.

Just like Harry. No complications, emotional ties or permanence. Vicky and Dilys were important to string along but they were dispensable. Vicky was particularly important because of Victor. Dilys had her uses but when they fulfilled their purpose they would be disposed of.

Julie had a strange start to life. A lovechild but in the middle of parents whom was hell-bent on greed. She had not seen much love and the only emotion was anger. This was the family life she had and with no one to live for, or to prove herself to, the prize was for the taking. All for her.

Clive, Robin, Harry and Victor were all out to out-do each other. Each had a slice of the action but now it was there. Drugs, booze, gambling and guns and links to terrorist groups, dealers and small part players like the CRU. The prize was great and the only obstacles were Victor,

Warlord and Harry. They were amateurs She would simply let them scrap it out and move in for the treasure trove.

Julie saw Harry as the main threat but she could soften him up with her charm. She looked forward to seeing him again but it would not be sentimental. But one last seduction appealed to her.

Vicky was impatient and Julie knew she could scupper any plans.

"Julie when are we goin' to get the loot?"

"Be patient Vicky. If we go running in we'll get nothing."

"Yeah, well I'm not sitting around forever Julie!"

Julie was irritated with Vicky.

"Listen Vicky, don't mess it up."

❧

The atmosphere in the club was of anticipation. Resembling the Wild West when two gun happy cowboys flexed their muscles in the saloon.

The downstairs lounge would normally be bubbling with local gossip and jokes. But it was a muffled din. There were whispers and a growing contempt for the three men in the corner.

Warlord and Harry's entry was greeted with cheers preserved for icons. Like heroes returning home from war.

"Good to see ya lads."

Bob Snow was glowing.

"I knew you'd be back."

"The scum over there thought ya were both dead … but"

"Thanks Bob. We'll have a drink later."

Warlord was soaking up the atmosphere

"Great, lads."

Harry looked around the room and his eyes hooked into the faces of Victor, Flashman and Pike.

"I need to see you Victor." His voice bellowed and with a glance like a rivet, there was a hush."

"Leave him to me Worrie."

Warlord felt the battle with Victor was his. A once loyal friend had betrayed him and he needed to get revenge.

Victor and his cohorts remained seated. They didn't flinch when Warlord came towards them.

Harry kicked the table to gain their attention.

"Are you listening to me."

With a sarcastic smile Victor stood up and confronted Warlord. They were head to head. Warlord sensed his superiority.

"Victor you're out of order."

"Worrie, what ya on about?"

"You Victor, trying to rip us all off!"

"Don't know what ya on about mate."

"What ya on about Worrie?"

Warlord couldn't handle words. He liked things simple.

He was incensed by Victor.

"You've been ripping us off, you know you have!"

"Worrie, you're imagining things mate."

Warlord was angry.

"You're no mate of mine Victor."

Harry was quick to react.

"Victor. Don't try to fool us. Enjoy tonight but don't get too comfortable."

Victor sat down and looked ahead of him. He then glanced at Harry.

"Alright, I'll cut you into the deal. You and all Worrie!"

Harry could smell a rat.

"What deal Victor?"

"Listen lads, I'm going back over to Spain tomorrow. Come over with me and we'll sort things out with Clive."

Warlord was not impressed.

"So as we can be shot at. No way!"

"Too many killings for my liking Victor."

"The CRU is not about murder. Deals yeah, cheap booze, tobacco but not drugs and guns."

There was a deathly silence.

"Guns, drugs, what."

Bob Snow had been deep in conversation with Kevin Robson, the steward and Trevor and Gary Blackstone. He was maturing in years, but his hearing was as sharp as ever.

"No place for you here Victor. Drugs is filth and guns is for the Americans!"

Victor stood up and looked around the room. He sensed that any friends that he might have had were starting to retreat.

"Aye Bob. Guns and drugs have kept the CRU going for a few years now. So don't be high and mighty with me."

"Ya lying Victor!"

"I'm not Bob and none of ya knew did ya."

Warlord was uneasy. Harry was ready to land a punch at Victor's ribs.

"Neither did I ya bloody liar."

Ya so bloody thick Worrie, ya didn't know."

Warlord's fuse burst but it was Harry who planted the first punch.

The scrap that followed resembled the spats that were common place in western movies. Chairs, tables, glasses anything else in sight were deployed. More than an excuse for a fight, which tested the patience of Kevin.

Kevin Robson was a quiet man usually but when he had to raise his voice he did with great effect.

"C'mon lads. Sit down and talk about it."

The shouting and crashing of wood and glass submerged his words.

Harry was in his element. He seized the moment because this was not only a fight but also a battle he would win.

Only Trevor and Gary Blackstone remained standing at he bar drinking. There was total mayhem. Even Bob got involved in the action.

Fighting poured out into the car park and side streets.

Harry grabbed Victor and pulled Warlord up off the floor.

"Ya gonna do what I say Victor Plumtree."

"There's no way ya gonna trick my mate Worrie or me."

"Where's the loot?"

Chapter 12
Closing in

The Police sirens were blaring. Outside on the street the fighting was clumsy, resembling a comedy. It was raining heavily. Water from passing traffic sprayed the fighters as they slogged it out. The two bodies were sliding all over the place and the fight was more of a fracas than a battle Locals had not seen the like for a number of years. The event was more than just a sideshow.

From across the road, close to the church Julie, Vicky and Dilys watched in amazement.

"Silly clowns."

Dilys had seen it all before working at the club for almost quarter of a century.

"Brawn but no brains."

For Julie it was a culture shock. It was quite a contrast to her privileged upbringing.

Vicky was for once quiet. There was anger in her face. Looking towards the village hall she saw Harry and Warlord flanking a forlorn

Victor. She wanted to shout abuse at him but she thought for once. There are more ways than one to skin a cat!

Harry had no intention of letting Victor out of his sight. Victor's return to Spain would not be how he wanted it. Harry knew that women were not part of Victor's deal but he wondered about Julie and also how long Francesca would stay behind bars. She would hire a lawyer and get bail. Francesca was mean and dangerous!

Clive was dead but he and Francesca had cooked up some plan. Victor had to know something.

Victor was nursing bruises. There were no broken bones and Victor's spirit was as strong as ever. But Victor wasn't stupid. He was cunning and Harry knew that. Money was his addiction.

Harry considered the odds of working with Victor and leading him into a trap. Warlord felt he should be taken as a hostage. He felt hurt by Victor's betrayal. But Warlord and Harry were a team. Harry would have his way.

~

Nardina's injuries were not life threatening. She longed for Harry to return to Benalmedina. Alone in hospital, her only visitor was Sanchez who talked about the hotel and business affairs. Sanchez was a friend but he did not inspire passion. Harry had ignited a flame that would never extinguish. The times with Harry were special and Nardina pondered, wondering if her lover would return.

Across town in a dark prison cell Francesca had tried to obtain her freedom by whatever means. Desperate, Francesca's bribes to lawyers included sexual favour and excessive amounts of cash.

For once, Francesca was not in the ascendancy. Her motives were quite different to her twin sister. Nardina's longing for passion and love was alien to Francesca who was desperate for power at any cost.

She had already committed murder. There was no remorse, just a chilling disregard for human feeling.

Francesca's mind was planning the next move.

The stirring body in the next cell was keen to provoke Francesca. Like any captive, there was frustration and the will to escape but also a desire to turn up the heat.

Julio Rodrigues was a former lover and her accountant. He wanted freedom more than anything else. But he knew Francesca and the influence she had. Being locked up for some scam he had not been involved in, Julio was incensed with Francesca who had set him up.

The way Julio worked was to charm Francesca and then to goad her on the missed opportunities she had had.

Rodrigues whispered to Francesca.

"Hey Francie, I bet I know where you'd like to be. Let's think….."

"In the arms of a man and making love I bet. Who could stop you eh."

Francesca was silent.

"What do ya mean Julio?"

"Yeah, I would like to love a man. What's wrong with that?"

888

Rodrigues hadn't realized how eager Francesca was. The cramped prison cell was not the elegant lifestyle she was used to. No fresh linen sheets but a customized cotton issue. Her sexual appetite was rampant.

The power and influence Rodriguez had was unrivaled by any other top ranking police official.

The pair had a hunger for conquest. Rodriguez had an idea.

"Francine, I can get these charges dropped. We can frame him for Clive."

"Who do ya mean Julio?"

"Your friend Harry!"

"Julio, you'd that for me."

"For both of us."

"I know the District Judge, Amelda. He owes me some favours!"

"This guy Harry Farmer tell me about him."

Francesca reeled off a tale that would impress any Judge and make a prosecution inevitable.

"I think it would be best not to frame Harry for murder but perhaps a serial rapist. He's been with some women and I'm sure we could get statements."

"Which women, Francie?"

"There's me of course, Julie and then there will be others on your files Julio."

"You're so devious Francie but….."

"A good idea Julio."

"Almost Francie but what about the murder. We need to get you off

The charge."

"You could say that Clive was the caring husband and he was out to get Harry and they got into a fight and Harry killed him. You can frame him Julio!"

"Leave it to me Francie. Stay calm and I'll be back soon."

"We'll sort things out in the morning with Amelda. Okay!"

"See you tomorrow Francie."

Rodriguez glanced at Francesca. Their eyes met and there was and evil fusion emerging between them.

The pair were determined to get the loot.

~

Harry was upbeat about a return to Spain. He was more eager than usual. Victor and Warlord they were a usual posse.

The stakes were high but so was the bounty.

Victor was an unwilling captor. He knew he was not the match for Harry physically and had difficulty handling Harry's mental agility. But Victor had his uses.

Harry wanted a lot of answers and also the whereabouts of the loot. His mind was ticking like a finely tuned engine.

Sitting in Warlord's cramped upstairs flat, Harry's interrogation began.

"Victor, we need a get a few things straight!"

"What's that Harry?"

"You need us, me and Worrie. If you run, you're dead mate."

Victor had lost Clive and things in Spain were in disarray. He feared Francesca and her ruthless deceptions. He knew of her associates and had met Rodriguez but he knew little.

"What do ya know about Francesca, Victor?"

Victor gave a puzzled look.

"How do ya know Francesca Harry?"

"Never mind that. But you know her Victor."

"Yeah, I do but…"

"But what Victor?

"Let me help you!"

Warlord stood up and walked towards Victor.

"I'll help you alright if you don't cough up Victor."

"Help you into the ambulance more like."

"Alright Worrie, leave it to me okay."

Harry was irritated by Warlord's interruption but could understand his frustration.

"Listen Victor. You can do this the easy way or I'll make it hard for you."

"What do ya mean Harry?"

"Just answer the questions, okay."

Harry raised his voice. He was becoming angry.

"Victor. You know Francesca because you know Clive and we know about Julie."

"So what?"

"We know you lied to them about Worrie and Dilys."

"I had to Harry."

Harry was increasingly irritated by Victor's stubbornness.

"I need to look after the CRU's interests!"

Warlord began pacing the floor.

"Don't be bloody stupid Victor. You sold us out."

Harry looked at Victor.

"Worrie's right. Put us out to dry and as for Vicky…."

"What about Vicky?"

Harry waited for a response.

Warlord was in like a flash.

"She thought you were dead and you will be when she finds you Victor!"

"Where is she now."

Victor looked worried.

"She knows all about you're dirty tricks Victor. So c'mon what's it all about?"

"What's in it for me Harry?"

Harry managed to block Warlord's verbal outburst.

"You'll get a cut I think."

"Aye, across ya face Victor."

Warlord's eyes were fierce with anger.

We're wasting our time Harry. He's givin' us nowt. Let's fill him in!"

"Wait a minute lads. I'll talk for a three way cut."

Victor looked desperate.

"Okay Victor, just talk."

Victor didn't press his case further.

"I've always suspected you Harry. Smooth talker and out for what you can get."

Harry resisted laying a punch.

But Warlord couldn't handle it and stormed out of the room.

"Go on Victor. Cut the crap!"

"You knew that Vicky and me stayed at the 'Rio Grande' and I got to know Clive very well. Just like you Harry."

"Clive had some connections. I must admit bootlegging booze was good trade but I didn't expect guns and that."

Harry tried to trick Victor.

"What guns Victor?"

"Some links with Arabs. Clive handled that side."

"So what did you handle Victor?"

"Me and Rodrigues, we managed the liquor side. Rodrigues is a top cop now but he was an accountant and we had things in common."

"Rodrigues, who?

"Julio Rodrigues. I met him first in Newcastle."

"Oh yeah, what was that about?"

"I really did want us to have the big break, the CRU."

" Awe Victor, you're too kind."

Warlord returned with some boxes of Pizza and garlic bread. He shouted to the two men.

"Thought we needed to eat, you and me Harry. Don't know about that bugger."

"Do'is a favour Worrie. Get some beer out of the fridge. We'll all eat Worrie!"

"Okay Harry."

Victor and Warlord didn't speak to each other but their stare cut through the air.

Harry didn't relent. He probed Victor about his business dealings with Clive and Rodrigues.

"So you had a deal goin' in Newcastle and me and Worrie were goin' to benefit. Really!"

"Yeah, but I knew what Worrie was like. He doesn't like going big!"

Warlord slammed his bottle of Kronenbourg hard on the table.

"There's such a thing as letting us know Victor. But I don't believe you!"

"Please yourself Worrie, but it's true."

Harry didn't want a fight. There had been enough of that in the last 24 hours.

"Okay Victor. So what was it about?"

"Clive, Francesca and her sister Nardina had some scam goin around the Med."

233

" Rodrigues and me were on the sidelines really."

Warlord perked up.

"Nardina. Wasn't that the lass we got out of that boarded up shop?"

Harry wanted to give Warlord a kicking.

"She knew too much and you were sniffin' around Harry."

"Or perhaps she had a conscience?"

"Remember Harry, Nardina and Francesca are sisters. Same blood and all that!"

"No she wanted more of a share. Too greedy for her own liking."

"Like and like eh?"

Warlord snapped. Victor's story was wearing thin.

"You can believe what ya want Harry. He's a bloody liar!"

"I'm not bluffin' Worrie. It's dangerous out there. They won't stop at anything. We'll be targets now."

Harry was thinking hard and fast. He was no quitter. There was no question that taking a risk was the only thing to do.

Victor would be the bait.

~

Judge Oscar Amelda was a youthful middle aged man. He had earned his title by a lot of hard work but his connections with the business community were lucrative.

As a lawyer, he had been successful as an advocate for wealthy criminals and was also a master of litigation. Politically, he was ambitious and had considered election to the Spanish parliament but he had far more influence in his home region. He had great flair and a popular figure.

No one suspected Amelda of foul play but he was addicted to wealth. He had been friends with Rodrigues for many years and had much to do with his career promotion. He had been a long time admirer of Rodrigues' skills in accountancy. But it was his ruthlessness he liked.

Sipping strong black coffee, he studied the transcripts of Francesca's prosecution. Amelda also considered her case citing Harry Farmer as a rapist and murderer. He was not convinced that the case against Harry was strong but he was not making judgement on a trial by jury. His task was to decide whether there was sufficient against

Francesca to keep her in police custody and enough in Francesca's statement to issue a warrant for Harry 's arrest.

Oscar Amelda was keen to present as a fair-minded Judge. He knew he had his enemies and he also realised the controversy of an arrest involving a British national. He was not inclined to make a hasty decision.

Francesca had been protected from the harsh prison regime. The police cells in Benalmedina's central police station were luxurious, in contrast to the severity of the state prison on the outskirts of town. It was vital to her that she got her freedom. She had heard nothing from

Rodriguez all day and wondered if there were problems or that he had double-crossed her. Francesca trusted no one!

~

A woman in the adjoining cell was screaming. The young female police officer taunted her.

"Signor Rodriguez has not come today eh."

Francesca did not answer.

"He's big friend eh?"

"Yes. I know him. Friends."

Francesca was feeling down. She didn't want to react to the taunts, even though the female officer was quite provoking.

~

Harry's phone rang. He had expected to hear from Natalie but the voice on the other end was distinctly Spanish.

"Hiya Harryee. When are you coming to see me?"

Harry was a bit taken aback.

"I don't know Nardi."

The airport pa system announced that the Newcastle to Malaga flight had been delayed by two hours.

"See you soon Harryee maybe. Missing you!"

Harry had things on his mind and as much as he fancied a night of passion with Nardina, he didn't want to lose sight of Victor.

Harry also recalled what Victor had said about Nardina. He didn't want too many risks!

Victor had told Harry and Warlord that it was Francesca who posed the greatest threat but this was no surprise to Harry. He knew too well the venom she portrayed.

But with Francesca locked up where was the money and who was controlling the purse strings?

Chapter 13
In for the Kill

Nardina did know that her twin sister was in police custody. But she doubted that Francesca would be there long. What she hoped and what she expected were quite different.

Francesca would somehow secure her release. She had amazing powers of manipulation.

And then there was Julie, vivacious but having the characteristics of her mother.

Nardina hated her sister for many reasons. As children, it was Francesca who achieved most. She bullied her way through school and in business she was tenacious.

When Clive and Nardina bought the Rio Grande, it was rundown. They made a success of it but lurking in the shadows Francesca lured Clive into an affair, mixing business and sexual pleasure.

The birth of their love child, Julie hurt Nardina. She loved Clive and longed to have children but Clive's infidelity put pay to that. Their relationship was shallow and Nardina's revenge was to be compensated for her loss.

Nardina knew the odds and the covert operation Francesca and Clive were involved in. They knew she could blow the whistle at any time.

But Nardina was greedy and her liaison with Harry was an obstacle. Clive knew Harry from their days in the Royal Engineers. He knew that Harry was shrewd and a mastermind. He saw Harry as a threat. Someone to have on side. But Harry couldn't be bought.

Robin, Harry's partner, was a soft target. Someone who was expected to come up with the goods but to achieve that he had to overcome Harry.

~

Harry mesmerized Nardina. She felt she could trust him. He excited her and had a passion, which Clive couldn't match. Seeing his face again brought elation.

Harry didn't see at first as he passed through the arrival terminal with Warlord and Victor. She didn't know Victor but had heard of him.

"Harryee, good to see you!"

Warlord didn't respond. His eyes were fixed on Victor. Harry glanced at Nardina. There was a gentle smile.

"What you doin' here Nardi?

"Waiting for you darling."

There were tears in Nardina's eyes. Her heart was beating fast as she hugged Harry, kissing him firmly on the lips.

Harry had missed her sparkle and vitality. A lot had happened in the last few weeks. Frustration and foiled by the tactics of the Benalmedina operation, Harry needed Nardina.

But any romantic interlude had to wait.

Victor had coughed up some information but getting to the bank was a main priority. Victor was a signatory to an account held in his name as well as Francesca and Rodriguez.

The banks were closed. The flight delay denied the trio the opportunity. With Francesca incarcerated, it was a question of whether Rodriguez had withdrawn or transferred the cash.

Victor, despite his financial skills never had a use for computers. Internet banking was not his scene.

~

Rodriguez had been elusive since his visit to Francesca. Judge Amelda had not made his decision. Certainly, Francesca had heard nothing as she sweated it out in her tiny cell. She was becoming increasingly irritated. Locked up, isolated and powerless. This was alien to Francesca.

The visitor she expected was to be male. It was difficult to hide her disappointment when Julie arrived.

Julie's visit was not concerned with her mother's welfare, more a fishing trip. Julie wanted a sniff of the cash and her mother had the authority.

"Julie, what you doing here?"

"I have some news for your mother."

"Victor's flown the nest."

"What do you mean Julie?"

There was no affection between the two women.

"Victor is with Harry and his side-kick. The guy I thought was Victor."

"And so, what does that mean?"

"Victor has probably done a deal with them two. They're all old friends, loyalty and all that."

"Victor can get the money, unless I get to the bank first!"

Francesca weighed up the options. Should she trust Julie over Rodriguez? Either way she could lose. But then there was Harry; he could take the lot.

"I have to get out of here Julie. You need to help me."

"I want to mother. I'll get the money on your authority. We'll split it 50-50 okay?"

"I'll decide that Julie, not you."

"I don't think you have much choice, mother."

The two women stared at each other. They were steadfast but common sense had to take precedence.

For once in her life Francesca was being controlled. She could feel an overwhelming capitulation. Being conciliatory was not her preferred gesture.

"Listen Julie. If I can get the authority I would like you to get the money I will see that you get what you deserve."

"I want 50 per cent mother. Nothing less, okay."

Francesca was angry but knew too well how she had brought up Julie to look after herself. It was starting to haunt her.

"Okay, Julie. Just do it. But I need to get the papers."

"I think I can help their mother."

Julie pulled a bundle of papers from a leather file. Got these earlier today!"

"Where from Julie?"

"Let's just say from a reluctant male."

"Who Julie?"

"Julio Rodriguez."

"Julio, how?"

"I paid him a visit and let's just say he was trapped into giving me the papers."

"You've killed him Julie, haven't you?"

"No he's not dead. Well not yet mother."

"Mr. Rodriguez thinks he knows a lot but I know more about him and his games. He was out to squeeze you mother. So you can thank me!"

"What do you mean Julie?"

"Rodriguez was making plans for a trip to the Caribbean. Single and no return ticket."

"You're making this up Julie, you have to be!"

"It's true mother, believe it."

Francesca could feel her world caving in on her. The years of 'wheeling and dealing', deception and scams were coming to an end. There was no guarantee that Julie had saved the day!

Francesca signed the forms.

"You'd better get going Julie. You need an early start in the morning."

There was no affectionate embrace.

The morning sunshine did little to please the pundits. Julie had booked in at a hotel close to the bank. Harry, with Victor and Warlord in tow were in a hotel a few blocks away.

It was Julie who got to the bank first. She was calm on the outside but her nerves were biting.

The young female bank cashier was efficient and pleasant. Julie just wanted to get down to business. The cashier examined the documents carefully and asked for proof of identity. She then went into her computer data bank.

"Signorita, there is a problem. The account has been closed. I'm sorry."

Julie was livid.

"Sorry. What do you mean? You are incompetent!"

The young cashier was resolute and was unaffected by Julie's outburst.

"I'm sorry signorita. I'll get a print-out of the account details for you!"

Julie gazed at the document, which showed that 'Costa Investments SA' was no longer. She didn't notice the three men entering the bank.

"Julie!"

Harry's voice rang around the reception area. He caught Julie at her most vulnerable.

Harry how are you?

"I'm fine Julie."

"What about you?"

Julie couldn't hide her shock and disappointment but didn't reveal anything.

"I'm in a hurry. I'll catch up with you Harry okay?"

"See you Julie."

As Julie turned around they both knew they shared the same desire. But Harry, Victor and Warlord also felt cheated. No funds and yet more questions.

"Bloody hell Harry what's going on?"

"Wish I knew Worrie."

"Victor you better not have duped us!"

Victor was a mystified as Harry and Warlord.

"I don't know where the money's gone. Believe me!"

"Believe you, you've got to be joking!"

Warlord was seething. Harry was keeping calm.

"Listen Worrie. Arguments will get us nowhere."

"Any ideas Victor?"

"Sounds like Rodriguez. Certainly Julie discovered the same as us and her mother's locked up."

"Anybody else?"

"No, I don't think so. Of course there is Nardina."

"But I don't think she could. Rodriguez is the one who could have done it."

"How do we get to him then."

Harry was eager and more determined now.

"Well, as a top cop it should be easy but…"

"Let's go then!"

A whole morning had gone by and Francesca had heard nothing. She was restless and felt rejected. Her worst fears were that Julie had gone off with the loot. But what of Rodriguez? He wasn't dead, according to Julie. Julio was a survivor, just like her. Had they signed a pact?

Powerless, her mind was spinning. She had to get out. But her destiny was in the hands of Judge Amelda.

Francesca had no one to turn to. Her lawyer had not been involved in the application by Rodriguez to Amelda. She had to play the waiting game.

Julio Rodriguez lived in luxury. For a public servant it was an extravagant life style but of course as well as being Police Chief he had had a lucrative career as an accountant.

Money was an addiction. Women and sex was an obsession.

Francesca was one of a number of conquests. He had never married but had his choice of admirers.

His third floor apartment was close to the town centre but in a stylish neighbourhhood. It was secluded and had sophisticated security.

There was little sign of life when Harry arrived with his posse. The front door was open and there was an array of memorabilia strewn across the floor. There were further signs of disturbance up the stairs. But nothing had been taken.

Rodriguez was lying beside one of two large leather sofas. He was unconscious but was breathing. There was an expensive feminine scent. Rodriguez had been drugged.

Harry managed to revive him. But his words were slurred.

Rodriguez glanced in the direction of Victor. The other two men were strangers.

"We need some answers Julio."

"What do you mean?"

Victor was keen to pursue some answers.

"Who are they?"

"Never mind, what happened to you?"

" Don't know but one minute I was talking to her and the next I can't remember."

"Who was she?"

"Sardinia, that's who it was."

Harry didn't know Rodriguez but there was something false about him. He was confused about Nardina but he didn't believe that she had been the culprit.

Rodriguez was now more alert and there was strength in his voice.

"I want you to leave now. You are not welcome."

" What would you do if I said I was going nowhere."

"Not until I get some answers Mr. Rodriguez."

Rodriguez and his frail attempts to eject the three men did not daunt Harry. He was not he most robust man and was no match for Harry.

"I think I need to introduce myself, Mr. Rodriguez and remind you that I am not going to take any crap from you."

Rodriguez swallowed hard. Warlord rubbed his hands in anticipation of a tussle. Victor's head was down.

"You need to ask Victor some questions. He was in this as much as anybody else."

"I know of you Mr. Farmer and I know about you and Nardina. You shouldn't underestimate her!"

"I am talking about you not Nardina. You have a lot to lose and believe me if you mess us around you will be more than a loser."

"You're threatening me Mr. Farmer, I don't like that."

" That's tough, cos' I am threatening you."

"The money's gone from the bank and I want to know where."

"Don't look at me. If there's no money in the bank I'm a loser."

"We don't think you are right."

Harry grabbed hold of Rodriguez and pulled him off the floor. Pushing him down onto the sofa he followed through a punch that winded the Police chief.

"You can have it or you can tell us what we need to know. One way or the other we're not goin' until we get some answers."

"I know nothing. Try Nardina. She will have the money!"

"What about Francesca. You and her are close yeah?"

"We have been. But she is locked up. Can't do very much can she?"

Victor and Warlord had enjoyed the tussle but they were restless.

Warlord was impatient.

"Let's go Harry. Getting nowhere here!"

Harry felt that he had scored some points over Rodriguez. They both knew that they would meet again.

" I'll be back Mr. Rodrigues, I'll be watching you."

As the three men left the apartment Rodriguez nervously grabbed his mobile phone.

~

Julie had gone into hiding. Although her mother could do little to invade her space, Dilys and Vicky were impatient and wanted their share. They were not ideal companions. The money was their only interest.

"I'm sick of being stuck in this place. It's too hot and them flies are all over."

"Not many flies in Coxburn I bet Dilys."

"No just the one's hovering around the bar in the club."

"That's if there's any club left after the fight."

"Don't worry Vicky, not even a nuclear bomb could shift that place let alone the punters. I'm 'sure some of them are permanent fixtures!"

"Yeah, you're right Dilys. Wouldn't mind goin' back if I'm bein' honest!"

"Me too Vicky."

"This Julie's done a runner and I don't know about you but I can't afford to stay."

"Me neither Dilys."

"Anyway, I think Harry will see us alright."

"Do you fancy him Dilys."

"Yeah, I think I do. Who wouldn't?"

"Well I have to say he's better looking than my Victor. Wouldn't say that to his face though!"

The two women laughed, as they planned their return journey.

❧

Nardina was soaking herself in the bath when the doorbell rang. Quickly wrapping her robe around her, she felt excited. She hoped it was Harry, as she eagerly opened the door.

She was not disappointed when she saw him. But he looked pre-occupied.

"Nardi I need to talk to you."

Harry's voice was stern.

"Harryee, it's good to see you."

As Nardina kissed Harry passionately, she did not feel that he shared the moment.

"What's wrong Harry?"

"Please tell me. We've always been honest with each other."

"Honest, yes. That's what I want you to be Nardina."

Harry's bluntness took Nardina by surprise.

"Nardi, where's the money?"

"Harryee, what do you mean. What money?

"C'mon Nardi, I'm not a fool!"

"Harryee, you know that I wouldn't take money unless it belonged to me."

"So you have the money?"

"Harryee, I have money from Clive, which I was due to but no other money."

Harry felt he needed to explain himself.

"Nardi, how much do you know about Clive's business dealings?"

"I know about him, Francesca and Rodriguez. They had big plans and I knew too much."

"You have to understand Harry I hated what Francesca and Clive did to me."

Tears rolled down Nardina's face.

"I was hurt and I they owed me a lot. More than just money."

Harry hung onto every word.

"Nardi, did you kill Robin and Clive?"

"Harryee, I couldn't kill anyone."

"I can hate and I can love."

"Do you know something Harryee?"

Nardina was sobbing. Harry wanted to console her but he wanted to be sure about her.

"What Nardi?"

"I love you."

Before Harry could answer her, she had loosened her robe and her naked body fell into his arms. If Nardina wanted to seduce Harry, he was easy prey.

They romped on the bed for a while before there was a loud knock at the door. Harry and Nardina were intense and ignored the interruption. But the noise got louder.

Harry clad in boxer shorts answered the door. It was the Policia and they had a warrant for Harry's arrest. The charges were for rape and murder.

The two policemen were determined and Harry didn't resist arrest. Nardina was distraught, screaming as Harry was led away.

There was nothing Nardina could do herself. She made a call on her mobile. It was to Julio Rodriguez.

Chapter 14
Taking Off

With Harry out of the way, Warlord was lost. Victor was relieved and felt a new lease of life. He had more in common with the attraction of the fast lane but there were risks.

Victor didn't realize it but to Rodriguez, he was small time. Once he had his uses but now he was surplus to requirements. Harry was more of an asset than Victor was able to accept. He was adamant that his new found friends in Benalmedina would do a deal.

The vultures had moved in and there was no room for dealers. The main players had the stage.

Harry was taken to the same Police station that held Francesca. If there was an attempt by his captors to break his spirit they failed to succeed. Harry was full of fire.

His spirits were high. He had been in many scraps and had survived in the most primitive surroundings.

Harry had guessed that Police Chief, Julio Rodriguez had sought some kind of revenge for Harry's intrusion and he would play his game.

Rodriguez was in familiar territory and had the backing of a summons signed by his pal, Judge Amelda.

Harry noticed that despite the advantage, Rodriguez was edgy. He was tempted to tease the Police Chief but thought better. Play cool and let Rodriguez take the pressure.

"Now Signor, Mr. Harry Farmer. You not so clever now eh!"

"Murder and rape. You are in real trouble."

Harry said nothing.

"Do you deny the charges?"

"What charges, Mr. Rodriguez?"

"Who am I supposed to have murdered or raped?"

"You murdered Clive and have raped a number of women."

Harry sensed the direction of the questions.

"Name the women then."

"Clive's widow, Francesca, his daughter Julie and that is a start."

"I think you have to prove it Mr. Rodriguez with evidence."

"I have statements Mr. Farmer."

Harry wanted a confrontation.

"I bet you have. Any witnesses?"

"I can prove you did commit these offences."

"Well prove it. I'm in no rush."

Rodriguez was uneasy.

"So you deny any charges?"

"Yes I do."

Harry was no lawyer but he grasped the nettle. Rodriguez wanted to carve up Harry and that was obvious. A lawyer would help but not just yet.

"Mr. Rodriguez!"

"Yes."

"I need all of the details of these so-called charges and I want a phone."

"A private phone."

"Okay!"

Rodriguez and his cohorts left the interview room and a phone was provided. Harry checked for any bugging device before punching in the phone number.

Warlord was at the hotel with Victor when his mobile phone rang out.

"Worrie, it's me."

Harry's voice was hushed.

"Harry are you alright mate?"

"No, they are trying to sting me for murder and rape. It's all a load of rubbish but I think I 'll. need a lawyer. Get hold of Jerome Chance will you."

"Yeah I will Harry, don't worry."

It was Jerome Chance who rang Harry within minutes of his call to Warlord. Harry didn't know the aging lawyer but he knew of his reputation through the CRU. He was mean but most of all he was a winner, whether buy fair means or not.

"Harry, Warlord's told me about your plight. I can help but I will need to involve a lawyer over there."

Harry was perturbed.

"Sorry Jerome. I trust you but any local lawyers might be under the Judge's control."

"Don't worry Harry. I am coming over there. I know some law firm in Valencia. I might use them. I should be with you tomorrow afternoon, okay!"

"Is there anything you need?"

"Yeah. To get out of here!"

"Sure. We'll get on to it."

"By the way Jerome I've asked them to give me the details of the charges."

"That's okay Harry. I would have been asking that myself as your lawyer."

"See you tomorrow."

Harry spent the rest of the afternoon and evening in his cell. Nothing to read. The food was warm and oily. He chose to catch up on some sleep.

Nardina had little success in getting hold of Rodriguez. Despite several attempts, Rodriguez had not returned her calls. She felt she needed to take more drastic action.

~

Jerome Chance arrived at the Police station at 4pm. He had been on the phone earlier to a law firm in Valencia. Chance was conscientious and meticulous with detail. He did not having a working knowledge of Spanish criminal law, but the principles were not that different. The strength of the evidence was the key. His main concern was Judge Amelda and had asked for some research. He had heard he had form and wanted to discredit him if necessary.

Harry was pleased to see Jerome. There was no time for small chat.

"What have you found out Jerome."

"Well Harry. It looks like these trumped up charges could stick, unless we can discredit the evidence." "What are the chances Jerome?"

"The people in Valencia say that Rodriguez and Amelia are buddies and a couple of mavericks."

"They just manage to keep clean but a few years ago there was a federal investigation. Fraud, money laundering and a sniff about drugs and links to terrorists."

"But they scraped through but they were not untarnished. No smoke without fire!"

"You know Rodriguez was an accountant, a former lover of Francesca. What we need to know is what part the Judge has in the business. I suspect he is up to his arm pits!"

Harry was becoming a little impatient.

"Where does this all lead to Jerome?"

"Am I going to get out of here?"

"There's a chance Harry. We need to piece you're whereabouts."

"I think the rape charges are a non-starter, it is the murder charge we need to concentrate on. We need an alibi Harry."

"In many ways it simple: where were you around the time of Clive's murder."

"I was all over the place Jerome."

"That's the problem Harry we need something more definite than that. How about Nardina?

"What do you mean Jerome?"

"Will she supply an alibi?"

"I'm sure she would but I don't want to involve her."

"Listen Harry, you are in a desperate situation. I would suggest we talk to Nardina. I'll go and see her Harry."

Harry felt he had to concede, but knew that the price was high. He wasn't totally sure about where Nardina stood.

~

Francesca's hopes were raised when she had heard of Harry's capture. She was sure that Rodriguez would seek her release now.

Francesca refused to accept that Harry would be the victor.

Rodriguez looked desperate. His facial expression portrayed a man being hunted. His smile did not reveal hope.

She didn't expect Rodriguez to show any favour in front of his colleagues but thought he might give her some hope. Francesca was desperate to get out and was not handling her confinement as well as Harry.

"Hello Julio. I thought you'd forgotten about me!"

Rodriguez was not good at handling bad news. He was even worse at deception.

"Sorry Francine, but you gotta stay in here a little longer."

"Why Julio?"

"I here you've got Harry. So what's the problem?"

"Judge Amelda does not work in haste. He wants to consider all of the facts."

Francesca was impatient.

"Really Julio. More like he wants to consider himself and knives in the back!"

Rodriguez looked worried.

"Be quiet Francine. I'm sure you'll get out of here. Be patient."

"Julio, you know I can't handle being locked up. I've been here for nearly a week. You promised me a couple of days, that's all!"

"Be patient, just a coupe of days."

Francesca was breathing heavily. Despair was setting in.

Rodriguez was sitting in his large office. He was a lonely man. His heart was sunk. He had learned that Jerome Chance was digging and was examining transcripts from the inquiry. He and Amelda had escaped by the skin of their teeth. They could ill afford mud in their faces!

Sunk in his leather chair, head in his hands, Rodriguez' phone rang out.

"Julio, its Oscar here. I think we need to release Harry Farmer."

Rodriguez was not surprised but hated being compromised.

There was silence.

"Are you there Julio?"

"Yeah, I'm here Oscar."

"Listen Oscar, I have an idea!"

"What Julio?"

"Let's hang in on Francesca and implicate Harry Farmer. They were having an affair. We're in the clear then."

"It's tempting Julio but we'd be found out."

"Francesca had the motive and is guilty I think. Release Signor Farmer."

"Sorry Julio!"

Rodriguez hated being beaten but self-preservation was important. Francesca would have to pay the price!

Telling Francesca would be difficult but putting it off would be all the more frustrating. He chose to take a woman officer with him to her cell. There were no sounds from within the tiny room. As the door opened, he felt a tug from behind the door.

The sheets were missing from the bed. Instead they were suspended from a hook above the door, providing a noose for Francesca's neck.

Rodriguez could ill afford to show emotion but tears lodged in his eyes. Looking at the stillness in Francesca's body, She had saved him from questions about their relationship and their business activities. But that was not her reason. Ending her life was the only possible course. Her pride and hunger for power had been broken.

The death of Francesca brought pressure for Rodriguez and an investigation would surely be ordered. The spotlight was on him and he felt trapped.

But unlike Francesca, Rodriguez would live and fight to the end. He would bring people down if necessary.

~

Harry felt upbeat. He had received a visit from Jerome and the news of his release, but there was added incentive: seeing Rodrigues losing his clutch for power.

With Rodriguez on the ropes, he thought hard about going in for the kill. But he didn't want to scupper his chances.

Certainly Rodriguez was the target. He probably had the money but perhaps adding some pressure and letting him sweat was the better option. Then there was Nardina.

Harry's more immediate priority was to see Warlord. Victor was less important now but could still be useful.

Jerome had had his easiest brief. Harry thanked him but believed that Jerome would be well compensated.

Harry had coped with his short spell in captivity but the scent of the morning greeted him. He fancied a long walk, not too rushed. Maybe breakfast on the way. His dreams were dampened for a short while by red tape!

A young Spanish guard appeared just as Jerome was about to leave. In a mumble of words, Harry identified with a few but could not keep up with the fast speaking

Spaniard. Much to Harry's amazement, Jerome had a grasp and interpreted.

"Harry, a little problem I'm afraid."

"They need your passport before you are released. I can get it for you."

"Is it back at the hotel with Warlord?"

"No they have it here Jerome. I'd just come from the airport when they arrested me. I bet Rodriguez is playing games!"

"We'll see Harry. If he is we'll have him!"

When Jerome inquired about Rodriguez, no one knew his whereabouts. Harry's passport or at least its disappearance was also a mystery.

Jerome did establish that Rodriguez had probably gone off somewhere along the Costa del Sol and after further prompting he discovered Rodriguez had some family living in Algeciras. Jerome sensed it was a ploy. Somehow he's get Harry out, via the British Consular in Malaga. Rodriguez could play his games!

It was Thursday evening and darkness had fallen. Any attempt to release Harry would have to wait until Friday morning.

Harry was incensed.

"What do ya mean Jerome, I have to wait for the British Consular. I'm innocent, stuck up in this smelly joint."

"Sorry Harry. We can't do anything without your passport or something that says your British. That's where the Consular comes in."

"But he doesn't know me, does he?"

"More bloody delay!"

"I need to get out Jerome, there are things to do."

"I know that Harry and I'll be as fast as I can. Promise."

Harry was unusually agitated. He had been fenced in before but not because of some bent policeman playing games. He was innocent and should be out there nailing him.

Sleep was not available to Harry most of the night. Shouting and screaming from the overnight trade of drunks and the stale smell of paella and coffee spilt out through the small window in his cell.

There was a commotion but not among the prisoners. There were loud voices but Harry couldn't make out the gabble of Spanish voices. Out of the din there was the solitary sound of two feet stomping along the marble floors. He couldn't make out whether it was a man or woman until the figure emerged from the shadows of the long corridor.

Nardina appeared like the morning sunshine. An array of bright colours shone in Harry's eyes. Her dark complexion vibrant and her black hair tied back, she was a determined woman.

"Harryee, what are you doing here?"

"I heard you got out."

Harry was sickened but pleased to see Nardina.

"I don't know Nardi. Rodriguez is playing games."

Nardina was prevented entry to Harry's pad but her scent was strong and their eyes met with meaning.

"I am going to get out of here Nardi, don't worry. There're things to sort out!"

"Harryee, I am sorting out the mess. I've spoken to my lawyer and he is with your man Jerome."

"Rodriguez has gone missing, but I think he knows there is trouble for him when he turns up."

"Harry have you heard of Oscar Amelda?"

"Yeah, I think so."

Harry was rubbing his eyes, still taking in what Nardina was saying.

"Why do you ask about Amelda then?"

"Rodriguez and Amelda are into something big and I think they have been found out."

"How do you know this Nardi?"

"My lawyer tells me but I know Rodriguez and know what he's like. Ruthless I think!"

"He knows your sister, doesn't he?

Harry didn't know about Francesca's suicide.

"You don't know about my sister, do you Harryee."

"The bitch, she is dead."

There was mixed emotion. Tears in her eyes that stirred up anger with some grief. There was over-riding revulsion that she directed at Rodriguez in particular.

"Rodriguez needs to be caught Harryee. He is evil!"

"Well you need to get me out of here Nardi!"

"I will Harryee but tell me something?"

"What Nardi?"

"Move in with me darling."

Harry relented, at least for the moment. He was desperate to get out of the stinking hole of a place.

Within the hour Harry was out and into the sunshine and bustle of Benalmedena. Nardina was close to him.

Harry had much to do. Getting to Rodriguez was a top priority and seeing Warlord. But for the moment being with Nardina was quite a rush of excitement. The morning was still young enough for the two of them.

"Let's go for a swim Nardi!"

"Okay Harryee. Then we make love darling, si?"

Harry smiled again, knowing he could enjoy some moments with Nardina. Freedom also meant he could seek revenge on Rodriguez.

"Let's go Nardi!"

The two lovers sped off to the beach and the thrust of waves.

Chapter 15
In for the Kill

Harry and Nardina had become close but for Harry being intimate was nice but anything permanent unsettled him.

Nardina was exhilarating. He enjoyed being with her and they shared a love that extended sexual pleasure. They admired the Andulician landscape, and the music. But they had a common goal - to beat off Rodriguez and Amelda.

Back at the 'Rio Grand' after a morning swim, the couple lay naked under the sheets. Whatever their intimacy meant, Harry and Nardina thought hard about the future.

"Harryee, let's go off somewhere after all this. Where do you fancy?"

"Nardi, there's a lot to do before we can go anywhere."

Harry needed to keep his feet on the ground. He wanted some time away but needed to nail the two Spaniards.

There was a loud knock on the door. Nardina rushed to open but Harry was more cautious. Holding her back. There were voices.

"Nardina. Can I need to speak with you."

It was Jose Fernandez, her lawyer.

"Wait a moment Jose."

Nardina got dressed. Harry had grabbed his attire on hearing the knock at the door.

Fernandez was in his late fifties. More of a father figure and loyal but his retainer ensured loyalty. He had watched Nardina and Clive's success. He had warned her of Clive's secret activities. She was always eager to forgive.

Like his client, Fernandez wanted revenge against his old adversary Amelda. They had been to law school together and had bitter rows. Fernandez worked hard in bars and restaurants to supplement his income, whereas Amelda was one of a generation of the legal dynasties that dominated the Spanish Judiciary.

Amelda held the view that the lower classes should never be allowed to succeed but particularly in Law. His family had supported the forces of Franco. It was about power and like General Franco, whose tyranny crushed the opportunities of the Spanish people for decades, Amelda wanted power for himself. If anyone stood in his way they would be dispensed with.

Fernandez knew of Harry, through meeting Jerome and thought of him as a chancer. He gave a glance to Harry but their eyes didn't meet.

"Nardina, we need to talk alone!"

"Jose, any thing you say, you say in front of Harry, okay!"

"Whatever Nardina but it concerns your friend."

There was malice in his voice.

"It's okay Nardi I need some air. I see you later."

She gripped his arm and they embraced.

"See you later darling!"

Harry thought he would look up Warlord. He hadn't heard from him since he got his freedom. Warlord's phone had been switched off.

Calling at the Los Domingo Hotel he learnt that his two cohorts had checked out. Back to England the young female receptionist informed him.

Harry pondered: with Warlord and Victor out of the way, he could handle the situation. At times, they were an obstacle!

He would give Warlord a ring later.

The dry climate, a blazing sun and dust in the air prompted Harry to have a couple of cool beers in the 'Coral Reef'.

He thought it would be nice to get away from Benalmedena once the business was done.

Nardina would enjoy Asia and the climbs of Katmandu. His mind drifted a little but the plan was foremost. He would make sure Warlord got his fair share and Victor might get something out of the booty. But for now Durham was furthermost in his mind. There was work to be done!

When he returned to the 'Rio Grande', he found Nardina sitting close to the bar. She could not hide her excitement.

"Hiya Harryee."

Harry noticed that Nardina had been crying.

"What's that lawyer been saying to you Nardi?"

"Oh, it's Francesca, she's dead. Killed herself."

"Jose says he thinks Rodriguez had something to do with it!"

"Probably Nardi. He tried to stitch me up!"

"You know that Francesca and Rodrigues were lovers Harryee?"

Wiping tears from her eyes, Nardina kissed Harry on the lips.

"You have a drink with me Harryee yes, si?"

"I hated Francesca but she is my sister."

"What else did Mr. Fernandez say to you."

"He said not to trust you Harryee but you know how I feel about you don't you?"

"What's he got against me then?"

"Oh, he is just looking out for me I think!"

"He is very protective and suspicious of the English."

"Oh really!"

"He also say that I have to be careful of Amelda and Rodriguez."

"I think we both know that Nardi."

~

Rodriguez had met up with his pal Amelda. They had a lot to worry about and to cover the cracks in their organization.

With the inquiry into their business affairs likely to expose everything, they had to plan a get-away. Rodriguez and Amelda were confident they could sink the likes of Harry and Warlord. Victor had been their pawn. He had now sided with the opposition. They still had a secret weapon!

Rodriguez mobile phone rang.

"Hiya Julio, how are you?"

"Just great for hearing your voice Julie."

"What's the news about Harry Farmer then?"

"It's bad for us Julie. He's out and alive!"

"Why, I thought you had it sewn up?"

"Never mind that Julie. We can squeeze him, now you have the money."

Julie didn't reply. There was silence, only Julie's slight breathing hinting there was life at the other end.

"What's wrong Julie?"

"Where's my mother?"

Rodriguez was not prepared for Julie's question.

"Yeah, I mean no."

Julie was impatient.

"What do you mean Julio. Is she alive or dead?"

285

"I'm sorry Julie, she's dead. Two days ago. Things got too much for her and she hung herself."

Rodriguez delivery was as clinical as a post mortem report.

There was rivalry between Julie and her mother, but there was some love.

Julie's tears and sobbing seemed genuine. She felt she had betrayed her mother. Not returning to see her with the money. The truth was she didn't have it.

"Julie, why not come over and talk."

"No, you bastard, you killed her. You killed her."

Julie's words rang in his ears.

"Listen Julie, I know you are upset. Please come over. We can sort this out."

The phone went dead.

Amelda was sitting across from Rodriguez and saw the strained look on his face.

"Need I ask, Julio?"

etsart.

"Ask what Oscar?"

"Don't play games with me Julio. We can't afford mistakes now"

"It's Julie, she's got cold feet!"

"Cold feet, what do you mean?

"She knows about her mother and blames me for it."

"Well that's true isn't it?"

Rodriguez looked angrily at the Judge. He would have like to have killed him but relied on him too much. They were two peas in the pod.

~

Harry was a little perturbed. He had tried getting hold of Warlord on his mobile. But the phone had been switched off. He tried once again.

The croaking voice sounded familiar.

"Worrie, is that you?"

"Harry, are ya alright mate?"

"Yeah, no thanks to you!"

"Harry, me an Victor were in jail. Some copper named Rodriguez had us arrested. Victor's still in there."

"Where are you then?"

"Some hole of a place above a bar and strip joint."

"That'll be right Worrie. Down your street!"

"Listen Harry, I'm not laughing."

"I'm been watched".

"Don't worry Worrie, I'll come straight over."

"Be careful Harry."

"Bloody hell, I thought things like this just happened on the telly!"

Harry wasn't particularly worried about Victor. He had his foot in both camps and so he deserved to it. Warlord was different. He was a mate.

Warlord's description of the accommodation was accurate. It was basic to the point that it had a front door, a couch, which Warlord occupied a small kitchen that was dark and dingy and a bedroom that was damp.

"What the hell are you din' here Worrie?"

"Had no money Harry. When they arrested me and Victor, they didn't give me the few Euros I had."

"You're not staying here mate, okay!"

"What's up with Plumtree anyway?"

"Don't know and don't really care Harry."

"Is he still with the cops then?"

"Yeah, I think so."

"C'mon Worrie, let's get you out of here. Come back with me to the 'Rio Grande'.

"Okay Harry but for how long. I'm gettin' sick of playing 'cat and mouse'!"

"Not for long Worrie, I promise."

As the two men left the shack, they both felt uneasy. A rush of anxiety mixed with the humidity.

Harry decided that a less conspicuous route to the 'Rio Grande' was advisable. If Warlord's worries were justified and more than just paranoia, they had to be vigilant.

Keeping off of the beaten track wasn't easy. Neither of them knew a direct route. So it was more a case of trial and error.

The evening sun had left an amber glow but darkness threatened.

Just as the two men were approaching the 'Rio Grande', a slender figure edged out of the shadows.

"Hello Harry. It has been along time."

"Where have you come from Julie?"

"More like the back of some rubbish, if you ask me Harry!"

"Well I'm not Worrie, okay!"

Julie smiled at the two men. She was sneering almost.

"I bet you haven't heard about Francesca?"

Julie looked puzzled. Harry wanted to be sincere.

"What about her Harry?"

"She's dead Julie. I'm sorry!"

Tears interrupted Julie's composure but Harry was not convinced that they were genuine.

"How do you know about her, Harry?"

"I think, you'd better ask Rodriguez that Julie."

Julie was surprised that Harry knew Julio Rodriguez.

"Can we talk Harry please?"

"What about Julie?"

Harry detected her engaging smile but he'd seen it before. He wasn't in the mood for giving sympathy.

"I don't think we have anything to talk about Julie."

Julie turned and walked away but her smile remained.

"If you change your mind Harry, give me a ring."

Julie pushed a business card in his hand.

"Don't bank on it Julie."

Harry and Warlord made their way to the 'Rio Grande'. Harry was convinced that Julie had come to deal. Why come to him unless she had problems.

The two men headed for the bar.

"Harry we need to get things sorted tonight!"

"Yeah you're right Worrie."

"I think I know just the person we can use?"

"Not Victor I hope."

"No, I think he's a liability Worrie."

"Who then?"

"Julie."

"Are you mad Harry?"

"No. I think this is what we should do."

"I've got her card."

The two men were enjoying a drink when Nardina heard their voices.

"Harryee, what are you up to?"

"Nardi, we need to get to Rodriguez and Julie is the way we get there."

"What do you mean Harryee?"

"Julie is dangerous, like her mother, my sister. She's all for herself."

"I know that Nardi but how do we get to Rodriguez?"

"Any ideas?"

"Yes darling. Me!"

You, I don't understand."

"I have the money Harry but to get the rest which Rodriguez and Amelda have stolen, you need me."

"But Nardi, why did you not tell me. I thought we trusted each other."

"We do Harryee. You must know how I feel about you. I was going to tell you but you've been there and everywhere."

Warlord interrupted

"That's true Harry. She's right!"

Nardina looked at Warlord and smiled.

"Listen the two of you and me can do this tomorrow."

"Tonight we need to eat and have some sleep."

"Okay Harryee and Worrie."

Warlord was fascinated by Nardina's voice. For the first time Nardina felt she was in control. She impressed Harry, even though he was annoyed she had not said anything about the money earlier.

The two lovers left Warlord at the bar eating chips and a burger and guzzling a bottle of 'San Miguel'

"Nite Worrie."

Harry and Nardina shouted in unison.

Chapter 16
New Horizons

Harry had not slept well the night before. Nardina was a great distraction but his mind was on Rodriguez. As he looked at Nardina sleeping he wondered why she could sleep. He was so pre-occupied, yet Nardina could take things in her stride.

The thought that Nardina had some control over his destiny held no threat. Harry planned to whisk her away after the coup.

Harry sipped black coffee. Sardine's slumber had ended. She was awake and curious about Harry's thoughts.

Nardina stroked Harry's neck and he was relaxed.

"Where do you think Julie is living Nardina?"

Nardina was surprised by his question.

"Why Harryee?"

"Just wondered."

"But Julie is of no use Harryee."

"I have the money and Rodriguez has the fortune!"

"So what about Rodriguez and you?"

"What do you mean Harryee?"

"I mean you both have the advantage, Francesca!"

"Harryee, I am Nardina, you know that. We made love last night."

"Can I be honest with you?"

"Yes, of course Harryee."

"And stop calling me Harryee."

"I'm Harry Farmer and you are Francesca Lomas aren't you?

"It is Nardina's body that wasted away in the Police cells. Nardina couldn't cope with being cooked up in there and she was desperate enough to kill herself."

"Isn't that right Francesca. You forged a plot with Rodriguez and it nearly worked didn't it."

"You make love like your sister Francesca. But there is a difference."

"Nardina was passionate and exciting. You are ruthless and entertaining."

"Like an actress. To you, life is a play; people are acting and manipulating. You're just evil Francesca!"

"You weren't saying that in bed last night."

"No, but for once I was acting."

There was a temporary impasse but the knock at the door surprised the pair.

Harry opened the door and Warlord's large frame fell towards him. He was unconscious but breathing. There was a note pinned to his shirt. It read:

"Don't mess with me Harry Farmer. Your days are numbered."

There was no name or hint of an identity but Harry knew the final conquest had arrived.

As he pulled Warlord around into an armchair, he kept an eye on Francesca. She was holding something shining. It was a knife. Her eyes showed venom. Her actions were immediate.

She lunged forward and forced the knife towards Harry's throat. He grabbed her arm and his physical force released the knife, which dropped to the floor.

Warlord was breathing heavily and was almost conscious. He held his hand against a bump to his head. He was ranting but not to anyone in particular. Still confused, his words were slurred.

"What's goin' on. Where am I?

"My bloody head hurts."

Francesca tried in vain to retrieve the knife but Harry's foot was firmly over the metal blade. Placing her hands around his neck, her long fingernails ripped into his skin. He forced her away and she tripped falling back onto the bed.

Being provocative was one of Francesca's characteristics. Harry was keen to keep his eyes on her, watching her every move.

Whatever evil she displayed there was no doubting her beauty. She used her sexuality with great skill.

Francesca had a skimpy nightie, which revealed her sexuality in full. She teased Harry but he was not inclined to submit to her charms.

"Harry, you know you want me."

"I don't want a scheming bitch and that's what you are!"

"Get dressed Francesca. We're going for a visit."

"Where?"

"Rodriguez and his Judge friend."

"What makes you so sure I will go?"

"Because if you don't you're dead!"

Harry's face had a fixed expression and Francesca was in no doubt as to his intentions.

Warlord was alert to what was going on.

"When are we goi'n Harry?"

"We're not mate!"

"You stay here okay!"

Harry's voice was strong. There was no compromise.

"But Harry we are mates and do things together."

"Worrie, we are mates but I need to do this alone."

"Don't argue, okay!"

Warlord didn't comment.

Harry picked up the knife and watched as Francesca dressed. Warlord chose to watch a football match on TV in an adjoining room.

Francesca wore a black dress, which suited her somber mood.

The drive to Rodriguez' remote hideout was not a pleasant journey. Harry insisted on Francesca driving. He watched her for any wrong moves.

Francesca did not give up her teasing of Harry, attempting to stop the bright red BMW convertible for some sexual pleasure.

"Harry, how about me and you."

"No chance Francesca!"

"I don't mean just sex but a deal."

"What deal?"

"How about 50-50?

"You're joking!"

"You need me Harry and you know it."

"Kill me and you get nothing."

"Really Francesca!"

Harry held the knife close to her right arm.

"Just keep driving and stop the small talk!"

Francesca was no push over; she was a survivor and would do anything for money and control.

"Okay kill me Harry, but you won't get the money."

"Do it my way and you get half of a lot."

Harry decided to play along with her. Nothing to lose but plenty to gain.

"Okay Francesca. No funny deals. Just me and you."

Harry's hands were firmly on the knife. There was no flirtation. It was purely business.

For Harry, Rodriguez was the target. Francesca was not the main feature. Whatever control she had, it was Rodriguez who held the cards. Secretly, he was anxious but displayed no outer signs.

The spider's web entwined with greed and deceit was about to be destroyed. Harry trusted his ability and had no doubts. He wasn't complacent though because he knew there would be more tricks and hurdles to overcome. But he could sense the prey!

The long drive in scorching temperatures neared its end. The high powered car was twisting its way up a dusty hillside track. Rodriguez' villa emerged out of nowhere. It was not surprisingly well protected, by a thick layer of trees around the perimeter.

The scent from the citrus trees mingled with Francesca's perfume as she got out of the car.

There were two cars in the drive; a black Audi TT convertible and a Mitsubishi Shogun, which looked familiar to Harry.

Harry judged the territory. He only had a knife. If there were weapons running loses, he would need to rely on combat. He held Francesca close to him, not for affection but as a 'cover'.

The house was large, spreading out over one level. There was no discrete front entrance. Access was on three points. It was quiet but for the chant of an assortment of birds.

Harry noticed an array of security cameras dotted along the side of the villa. He made for the side entrance and heard a familiar voice.

"Hello Harry. You look great!"

Glancing at Francesca the young woman turned. She had a gun in her hand.

"Nice to see you mother. I see you brought Harry along for the ride."

Francesca pretended to ignore her comments. Harry looked hard at both of them and made a dash for some bushes. The two women were an obvious ploy, in an attempt to soften Harry. It didn't work. He searched for the main man.

Harry felt a gush of adrenaline. Just like combat and jungle warfare, his enemy was hidden but he would seize on the scent.

As Harry made his way to the other side of the house crouched but keeping his eyes and mind alert, he saw an open patio door.

Lurking close to an olive tree he saw some towels strewn over a grassed area. There were voices and laughing from beyond the doors.

Harry decided to tease out the prey.

"Rodriguez, I know you are in there."

Rodriguez emerged with Amelda. Both men were armed. There was a burst of noise overhead as a helicopter hovered.

Harry remained motionless but not for long. Rolling into some bushes, he used the territory to his advantage. He had a dark green short sleeved shirt, which clung, to his body. Camouflage was difficult.

Harry was surrounded. The helicopter followed his movement. But Harry cast his eyes towards an outbuilding. He had to scramble and sprint to the open door. A ripple of bullets followed his path.

Inside Harry couldn't believe his eyes. There was immediate darkness following the glare of the strong sun. When his sight recovered he saw an arsenal of weapons.

Rodriguez had set a trap. The place was riddled with explosives. Strapped to one of four pillars was a woman. She had been drugged.

Harry rushed over to Natalie. She didn't respond and he could hear a ticking noise close to her.

It had been two months since they had met. Harry assumed she had gone back to London and got caught up in work.

His long-term girlfriend had made an emotional farewell. They had promised to go away for a long break. Now Harry was looking into Natalie's eyes. He wondered how they had found themselves in the grip of danger.

Just as Harry tried to untie Natalie, he heard a loud bang which was coming from outside. Above them there was vibration.

A top section of wall close to the roof collapsed and some debris fell.

Harry managed to grab a rifle and handgun. Quickly checking if they were loaded, he hauled Natalie over his shoulder.

Rushing to the door, a heavy blast of fire raced across him.

Harry dashed for the house. The early evening sun cast shadows. In the background the outbuilding exploded in a glow of amber.

Natalie had not gained total consciousness, but she was trying to speak.

"Nat, it's me. Don't worry we'll get out of here. Stay calm."

Natalie was trembling.

"Harry, be careful."

Harry was all too aware he had to be careful. A small army was after him. He'd escaped their first trap.

Entering the house, he heard shouting.

"Now signor, Mr. Farmer would you like a drink."

The dark figure appeared.

"We are not very good hosts are we?"

Harry looked straight into Rodriguez eyes. It was Rodriguez who responded first.

"You're a brave man Harry Farmer!"

"I agree!"

The other man close behind Rodriguez was unknown to Harry.

"Let me introduce myself. I am Oscar Amelda. I think you can do a job for us Mr. Farmer."

Harry weighed up the two men. They were calm. He was sweating heavily but his nerves were cool.

"What sort of job?"

"You could run our military division."

Harry looked curious.

"I thought you were a policeman, Mr. Rodriguez?"

"I was but I've quit."

"And who are you?"

Harry's eyes were fixed on Amelda.

"I see you like to know everything Mr. Farmer."

"Answer my question please."

"I am a Judge but Julio and myself are in business now."

"What's your poison Mr. Farmer?

"That is what you English say, yes?"

"You probably know. It would seem that you have done your homework."

"Julio get Harry a vodka and ice!"

Harry was not in a trusting mood. But he fancied a drink. Natalie was by his side.

"We are sorry about your lady but we needed to talk to you."

"Do you think I'm stupid?"

"You knew I was going to come here."

"Yes Mr. Farmer but just think a minute. A woman is a great attraction and a test to your concentration."

Harry was annoyed but kept cool.

"Okay. What's the deal then?"

"Not so eager Mr. Farmer."

"There is no deal. A job, a good job!"

"Every job has a price Judge."

"My price is £1 million."

"I think you can afford that?"

"You're right Mr. Farmer, there is a price for every job."

"But you need to work for us."

"Doing what exactly?"

"We have some military operations in a number of third world countries. In Africa we are fighting off military junta and in the Baltic States there are still factions at work."

"Your military career is something we know about. Also, you are a cool character. Not like that very English and greedy Victor Plumtree."

"He lacked adventure and was small-minded!"

Privately Harry agreed. Victor was good at figures but military junta was something Victor had little idea about.

"You're in a different league Mr. Farmer."

Harry privately was excited but didn't trust his potential employers. He knew of their shady dealings. Jerome Chance had told him about the Spanish Authorities' suspicions. But with a £1 million pay off, paid in advance, he could hold out for more. If the whole operation failed, he could take the two men with him.

How could he sell it to Warlord and the CRU?"

The money and the promise of more could appease them. A story that would excite the likes of Bob Snow, Dilys Palmer and the rest of them, making Harry the hero, appealed to his super-ego.

Harry believed that he could take on the assignment without any risk to himself or to anyone else. Natalie was far less comfortable but believed Harry. She was also attracted to the financial windfall Harry would receive.

Amelda and Rodriguez believed they had their man but Harry wanted to negotiate and there were certain conditions. Thinking that Harry would be easy to please was a wrong assumption to make.

Harry's plan was quite simple: he would accept the £1 million and play along with the game. He didn't believe that they would seriously trust him with their military operations, if indeed they existed.

For the moment, Harry needed a holiday, the one he promised himself on a Greek island. But that was for another time. Asia beckoned him and another challenge.

Climbing Everest seemed a dream a year ago. The events of the last few weeks: what started as a last deal for the CRU and ended with murder and deception did not foil Harry. He was now in a different league but this did not threaten him. It gave him impetus.

Chapter 17
Destinations Unlimited

Harry agreed to talk. Long into the night the three men discussed

the deal that would make Harry an instant million. But he had many questions for Rodriguez and Amelda.

Where were Julie and Francesca in all of this?

He told the two men of their scheming and their attempts to swing a deal with him. If he was dealing with anyone, it would not include them.

Harry insisted that the advance of £1 million would be paid into an account in the Bahamas. He would want that cleared in his account before going on holiday.

"What guarantees will you give to us that you won't cut and run?"

Rodriguez knew that Harry was a smooth operator and could opt to go underground.

He also knew that Harry had some loyalties, particularly Warlord and that if anything was to happen to him he would be hurt.

Harry watched the two men closely.

"I'll give you my word. Four weeks from today I will come back and I will start working for you."

"No, Mr. Farmer, how about this!"

"We pay you £100, 000 today and the balance will be paid into your account in one month."

"Then what guarantees have I got that you won't keep your side of the bargain?"

After haggling and threats and more negotiation, a deal was struck.

The three men knew there was a great deal at stake. Harry knew too much. They could bump him off but there was a desire by the Judge and the Police Chief to have Harry on board. He knew military installations and had operational knowledge of Europe and the Middle East. They all had much to gain.

"Okay Mr. Farmer. You get £500,000, now and an immediate cash advance of £100,000 and the balance in a month. That's a deal!"

The three men shook on the deal and Harry headed for the door with Natalie.

"Oh yes, before I go. What of the two scheming bitches"

"They cannot be trusted!"

"What do you suggest Mr. Farmer?"

Amelda looked straight at Natalie who had a confused look on her face.

Harry looked up at Amelda and Rodriguez. He smiled and considered their dilemma.

"You misunderstand Judge, They need to be disposed of, or I will…."

The door burst open and Francesca appeared with a handgun.

"I've listened to all the rubbish you have talked about. One million pounds and you have fallen for that Harry?"

"I thought you were intelligent. Taken in by two desperate men."

"Shut up Francesca!"

"Remember, we can get rid of you!"

"Really, I have the gun and I can kill you at any time.'

Harry made a surprise move.

"Just do it then, but I'd watch your back."

"I find guns are only as good as the person puling the trigger!"

Francesca and Julie were together. They looked to Amelda and Rodriguez for reassurance.

The two men had no use for them. They needed bloodsuckers less than someone with some military know how.

"Julio, we have had so much and we can..."

"No sentiment Francesca. Business and pleasure doesn't mix!"

"Forget her Rodriguez, I can help you."

"Two ruthless women eh!"

Amelda threw up his hands.

"We need you both like a hole in the head."

"Well maybe that it was what you are goin' to get."

There was a scuffle. The two women vying for position. A bullet rang out.

Instinctively, the three men hid for cover. Harry dragged Natalie with him. One of the women fell to the ground.

A further two bullets rang out. Harry held Natalie close. There was blood oozing from a leg wound. She was frozen with fear but was breathing.

As his eyes spanned across the room, he saw Julie lying with a fresh head wound. She was motionless. Julie lay on the floor close to the door between the lounge and hallway.

Rodriguez had disarmed Francesca and she looked up at Harry. He thought, even in capture she looked sensuous. Her eyes were fixed on him. She portrayed danger and passion. Two ingredients Harry liked in a woman.

Francesca was a distraction; an attractive woman but she could complicate Harry's complex life.

He looked down at Natalie. She was foaming at the mouth. Her injury didn't appear to be serious but she was having a fit.

Harry was not sure what to do. Having a bedside manner was not his usual routine.

Rodriguez helped Harry place Natalie on a sofa. She was breathing heavily. Blood was pouring from her lower leg. Rodriguez dashed to the kitchen and brought some liniment and bandage. He could sense Harry's anxieties.

Julie looked quite dead but no one seemed to care. All attention was on Natalie.

Francesca came forward. Her sense of caring was as genuine as her character. Her outreached hand touching Harry's shoulder was discarded.

Harry didn't comment but his swift rebuke spoke volumes.

Natalie began to breathe easier and her tolerance was stronger. Her dislike of Francesca was evident.

"What are you looking at?"

"You might look smart but you don't impress me."

"You' re a killer!"

Natalie's outburst surprised Harry. She was not usually reserved but taking on Francesca was a courageous move.

Francesca had never been attacked, verbally or otherwise. She was a bully and a perpetrator. She was not prepared for Natalie and seemed numb in her response.

Natalie let fly at Francesca. Two women fighting like men. No hair pulling, punching fists and feet kicking.

The pain Natalie was feeling from her wounds was quite visible, as was the strength of her hate.

Harry was not inclined to intervene. He was relishing the battle and saw a fighting spirit in the woman he loved.

Natalie had Francesca on the deck and she drew blood. But it was a controlled attack. She withdrew only because she was not a murderer.

Bruised physically, Francesca's pride was torn. Her heart and mind were ripped apart.

Harry agreed to meet with Rodriguez the following morning. His priority was to seek medical attention for Natalie.

The deal was done. Only some minor details to sort out. The three men agreed to meet the following morning. Rodriguez would drop Natalie and Harry off at the hospital and collect Harry for a meeting with him and Amelda the following morning.

Natalie's wounds were not serious. It was the trauma that caused the fit. Soon she and Harry would bask in the sun. Katmandu would wait for a few months.

Greece, the whitewashed houses and the sun drenched beaches and coral seas sounded and looked a perfect prospect.

Harry rang Warlord, who was confused by Harry's account of events. The news of the financial deal was a sweetener.

"How much Harry/"

"Can you cope with £250,000?"

"Bloody Hell Harry!"

"What about the others?"

"Who Flashman and Pike?

"Yeah."

"What do you think Worrie?"

The two men laughed.

"Give them a few thousand each. That's more than they deserve. But they can't say they didn't get nowt."

Harry had mentioned the deal but not the details.

"Will you be alright Harry?"

"You know me Worrie."

"I'll give you a ring when I get to Greece."

"Is it hot out there Harry?"

"Yeah, as hot as chip pan fat Worrie!"

"Why not come out for few weeks."

"We'll see Harry. I need to get over Spain first."

"Sure Worrie."

"You'll have the money at the end of the month. Is that okay Worrie?"

"Aye, no problem mate."

"Give Dilys, Kevin, Bob, Gary and Trevor my best. I'll come over to see them soon."

"Be sure you do Harry. Take care.

Harry felt he had done enough. He would probably see Warlord some time but there again he might not. They were friends but that was where the similarities ended.

Harry thought of Warlord. In a few weeks, he would enjoy being the centre of attention in the village and his beloved club. Going abroad was not something he aspired to. To him, food was simple; culture was football, darts and beer.

Thinking of Greece, it was not just the beauty of the place that fixed in Harry's mind. His thoughts were of sun and of his girlfriend Carla sunning herself. Having fun. Living for the moment.

Natalie was important to him but he was addicted to women. She was a chapter, not the whole book!

Life was an adventure and there were many more adventures to come.

Tomorrow he would be in Greece; Asia would be the destination in the next few months. Dreams would come true and whatever the fortunes from Rodriguez and Amelia, Harry would direct his own destiny.

Printed in Great Britain
by Amazon

17187306R10194